Power
Grind

STREET WIZARDS: BOOK THREE

Power Grind

by Troy Bannon

A YEARLING BOOK

Published by
Dell Publishing
a division of
Bantam Doubleday Dell Publishing Group, Inc.
666 Fifth Avenue
New York, New York 10103

The trademark Yearling® is registered in the U.S. Patent and Trademark Office.

The trademark Dell® is registered in the U.S. Patent and Trademark Office.

ISBN: 0-440-40559-9

Published by arrangement with Parachute Press, Inc.

Created by Robin Hardy

Printed in the United States of America

January 1992

10   9   8   7   6   5   4   3   2   1

CWO

**For Rod Philips,
best fresh cut on the pipes**

1

Petey Marino kicked down on the tail of his board and dragged to a sliding stop, tweaking the move by hauling around in a grinding 180 in the wide valley of the ramp. Above him, on a tall extension ladder propped against a light post just outside Ramp 2, Tom Garcia was tying off the fourth corner of a huge banner, which he had hung between two posts.

"Looks great, dude!" Petey shouted to his pal. "But we don't really need a sign—everybody in the world already knows about it," he added, staring up at the bright reds, greens, and blues. The banner read:

MEGARAD!
Radlands' Statewide Ramp and Freestyle
Competition
San Carlos, California

"I hope they've got my name engraved on that freestyle trophy," Petey shouted to Tom. "That way I won't have to have it done after I win it!"

"You're welcome to it, dude," Bobby Clark laughed, wheeling up next to Petey. "This competition's all about *ramping*, not street hot-dogging. Wait until you see the move me and Tom worked out! It'll blow you away—guaranteed!"

Tom, Petey, and Bobby were three-quarters of the skateboarding gang called the Street Wizards. Jordan Kowski, the fourth member, hadn't arrived at the park yet. Radlands was the gnarliest skateboarding park in southern California.

Petey grinned at Bobby. "You just don't give up, do you? Look, I'm not saying ramping isn't rad, but freestyling is what skateboarding's really all about. Freestyling's the heaviest . . ."

Petey was cut off in midsentence when a skater with long blond hair shot past. He slashed straight up the ramp, rolling hard, and crouched low on his board.

"The dude shows some class," Petey said, watching for the guy's next move. "You know him?"

"No," Bobby answered, looking around the skate park, which was more crowded than he had ever seen it. Skaters had been pouring in to San Carlos to practice on Radlands' half-pipes. "Before they announced the competition, we used to know every skater who came here. Now, we don't know half of them."

Climbing down the ladder, Tom paused to look into the ramp. The skater cranked his board back down from the coping, pumping for even more speed.

"Look at that T-shirt," Petey said. The skater wore bright red shorts and a bright red T-shirt, and his helmet, kneepads, and elbowpads were red, too. The dude's T-shirt had a stencil of a pair of sneakers on the back, over the words DIGGER SNEAKS. Under the shoes was a patch that read PRO.

"Outtasight," Bobby said. "Must be great to be sponsored by a big L.A. company like Digger Sneaks."

"Must be great to be sponsored by anybody," Petey answered. "Look at the dude's pads and helmet—they look brand-new. I could truly dig skating all over California with somebody else footing the bill."

Everyone's eyes were on the Digger Sneaks pro. His long blond ponytail streamed behind him as he rocketed up the ramp, his arms and his legs a deep, dark tan, his grin a flash of brilliant white. He was riding low once again, his momentum hot and his speed radical. He shot straight up past the coping, looking as if he'd never stop. His left hand snatched the lip of his board, holding it snug against the soles of his Diggers, his right hand clamping down on the coping in a death grip. He tweaked the handplant until he was a heartbeat away from a stall, then dropped toward the coping by collapsing his right arm. He threw himself back into the air, doing a full backward roll and landing on his wheels. He fired back down the ramp in a scorching fakie.

Cheers broke out, along with clapping, whistling, and rebel yells.

"Dynamite move!" Petey shouted.

"Yeah," Bobby agreed. "You don't see skating like that on the streets and sidewalks. Hey, there's Chelsea! I want to talk to her. I'll see you in a few minutes."

Petey watched Bobby skate over to where Chelsea McIntyre, leader of the all-girl gang the Shooters, had just wheeled down the ramp. Petey pushed his sweat-dampened dark hair off his forehead. Bobby, leader of the Street Wizards, was a top boarder, and though he was only twelve, he could outskate lots of dudes who had three or four years on him, at least on the ramps. Petey, at age eleven, was as hot on the streets as Bobby was on the ramps. He wished the Street Wizards would spend more time freestyling.

Petey shook off the thought and dropped into

4

the half-pipe gathering speed in the valley, cutting around and between other skaters. He arced halfway up the slope and cut back down, rolling well. The buzzing whirl of his wheels beneath him sent a very familiar tingle up and down his spine. He pumped hard and fired up the opposite slope; the breeze felt cool against his face, arms, and legs. He angled the nose of his board at the right moment, tromped on the tail, and laid his front trucks on the coping. The grind was hot, and it felt great—his balance was perfect, and he was relaxed and easy on his deck.

Petey croaked the grind just before he would have lost momentum, and wired a fakie back down the slope, swinging wide around a fresh cut who was lumbering along, fighting to stay on her board. The dude sponsored by Digger Sneaks called out, "Awesome grind, man! And a real smooth fakie. You're looking like a pro!"

Petey waved his thanks for the compliment. "When I can slam a move like you just did, maybe I will be a pro!"

"Nothing much to being a pro," the guy said, laughing. "All you gotta do is forget about sleeping or eating, practice thirty hours a day, and have your skin turn to hamburger from road rash, and you'll be there!" After a moment, he added, "Of course, it helps to be crazy, too."

"Then I'll get crazy." Petey laughed, but the pro was already skating off. As Petey was about to shove off again, a girl skater jammed up and snared a cool sliding stop.

"Like, a real heavy grind," she said with a bright smile. She was older than Petey—maybe sixteen or so—and she had the clean, healthy good looks of the surfer crowd. But she wasn't a surfer. She was a skateboarder with a sponsor. The back of her sweatshirt read CHEAP HAROLD'S BOARD STORE, and under that, PENNY KETCHUM, PRO.

"Thanks," Petey said. He noticed her board was a custom job, with a wider-than-normal nose and a little flip at the end of its narrow tail. It was decorated with Cheap Harold's decals, in screaming reds and yellows.

"My name is Penny Ketchum," she said. "You want a T-shirt? Harold's setting up a table over by the entry gate, and he'd dig any kind of advertising you could give him."

"Sure," Petey replied. His smile got even broader and his chestnut eyes twinkled. "But it would just break the hearts of the other Street Wizards if I was the only one with a Cheap Harold's shirt. It wouldn't be fair to the rest of my gang, you know what I mean?"

"OK, OK," Penny said, and laughed. "If your friends' moves are as radical as yours, you can bring them over later. You'll all get free shirts."

6

After she had skated off, Bobby and Chelsea rolled up. "Who's that girl?" Chelsea asked. She was dressed in hot-pink shorts and a hot-pink T-shirt, and her gear was hot pink, the Shooters' trademark.

"Her name's Penny. She's a pro for Cheap Harold's." Petey grinned at Bobby. "Guess what, dude? If we stop at the Cheap Harold's booth later on, we all get free T-shirts." He looked down at the shirt he was wearing. "Just about time, too. This one's getting a little rank."

"Getting a little rank!" Bobby exclaimed. "That shirt was rank the day I met you—about a thousand years ago!" He shook his head as he watched Penny talking to some skaters. "You know, that sponsorship thing is great. Can you imagine the Street Wizards with a sponsor, going all over the place handing out shirts and skating up a storm?"

"I really think you dudes are heavy enough to snag a sponsor," Chelsea said. "Petey, you're as hard as steel on the streets, and Bobby and Tom can burn ramps." She hesitated. "And Jordan, he's . . . uh . . . a really nice dude. I mean it. He's smart and friendly and . . . real nice," she repeated lamely.

Petey and Tom smiled at one another. It was no secret that Jordan wasn't a top skater.

"Maybe one day we'll latch on to a sponsor," Bobby said. "But there are so many board-crazy kids in San Carlos, it's tough to stand out from the crowd."

"All we need is some way to . . . look out!" Petey yelled. A fresh cut, pretty much out of control, swooped between Petey and Chelsea and banged into the tail of Bobby's board. Bobby went down on his knees, his pads taking the shock, his board scooting off riderless for a few yards. The fresh cut wiped out, too.

"Sorry, man," he said as he got to his feet and rushed to fetch Bobby's board. "I was riding the slope real good and not bothering anybody when . . ."

Raucous laughter cut the boy off. Scott Longo, the fourteen-year-old leader of the Pipe Riders, stood on his board nearby, grinning arrogantly. "How come every time I see a Street Wizard, he's checking out the pavement real close? Can't you dorks stay on your boards yet?"

Brad Munson, another Pipe Rider, slapped Scott on the back. "Only difference between Petey over there and that fresh cut is that the fresh cut's board looks new!"

Petey's face flushed bright red. "You want to skate against me sometime? All you use your board for is a chair while you watch everyone else skate!"

That remark got to Brad—because it was very close to the truth. He was the Pipe Riders' poorest skater, but he had the biggest mouth. "A skate-out or a punch-out, dweeb, I don't care which one! Any time, anywhere!" the Pipe Rider shouted.

"How about right now, turkey?" Petey stepped off his board and clenched his fists. Tom skated up in a hurry and grabbed Petey by the shoulder. "Chill, dude," he said. "You know fighting will get you canned from Radlands. And Brad isn't worth your trouble."

Bobby stepped over to Petey and Tom. "He's right, Petey. Brad's just a dork."

Petey continued to glare at Brad, then looked away. Brad and Scott rolled away laughing. Petey shrugged. "You guys are right. Munson just gets to me every once in a while, you know? I know he's a dork and a chicken. I shouldn't let him tick me off."

"Yeah," Bobby said. "Brad gets to everybody once in a while—not just you."

"Hey," Tom said, "who's interested in a free burger and all the Coke you can drink?"

"Where'd you get the bread?" Petey grinned, having already forgotten the incident with the Pipe Rider. "You're usually hitting us up for grub money, which none of us can figure out because Dan the Man pays you bucks deluxe." Tom worked part time at Radlands, whose owner was Dan Lyons.

"If I make such big money, how come I have holes in my sneaks and my board is so old my wheels are almost worn down to the axles?" Tom asked, laughing. "But the burgers and drinks are free. After I put the banner up, Mr. Lyons introduced me to a dude who's sponsored by Eddie G's Skater Supplies. He told me to bring you guys around to his table later to chow down."

"Great!" Bobby said. "Let's do some skating now and build up a thirst and an appetite. There's some heavy skating going on. If we're going to snag some trophies, we've gotta be truly awesome. And if we look good enough at the competition, maybe some honcho will offer us a contract."

"Yeah, right," Tom said. "Just as soon as my dog learns to fly."

"No, really, it could happen," Bobby said seriously. "All these pros around here had to be seen by somebody before they hooked up with their companies. We've got a radical shot at being scouted. All we have to do is burn the ramps in front of the judges."

Petey shrugged. "I guess that lets me out, then. I don't have a chance in ramp stuff. I'm just wheelin' here for chuckles. I need to concentrate on my freestyling-mile-high ollies and radical grinds and stuff. Yesterday I hung this acute power grind on the railing at the library."

"Mrs. Griffith will give you something acute if she catches you grinding her rail again." Bobby laughed, picturing the heavyset head librarian chasing after Petey.

Petey shrugged again, his eyes now lively with mischief. "She's just jealous of me 'cause she's too wide for a skateboard—she'd need a garage door with solid-steel wheels!"

The boys skated out from the quiet end of the valley, threading among other skaters. Petey looked around. There were out-of-town skateboarders everywhere, many of them with pro patches on their shirts. He snaked up and down the slopes, waiting for space to open up in the valley. When it did he was ready. He kicked the setting up for an olly. He was rolling hard, wheels buzzing, as he swung to his left to follow the line of the valley. The speed felt great. Then he eased the weight from his left foot, keeping his balance tight. Finally, he stomped down hard on the tail of his board and felt the quick burst of excitement he always felt at the start of a good olly.

His soar was long and high, and he touched down as surely and smoothly as a pouncing cat. The fresh cut who had knocked Bobby off his board raised his fist in a salute. "Radical, dude!" he shouted.

An hour later, Petey had laid down some prime

ollies, but he just couldn't get into practicing ramp moves. He placed a few long grinds on the coping, then started wheeling around, joking with friends and having fun. Chelsea noticed his grin and, swinging up next to him, joined him in a straight-down run into the valley.

"What's the smile for, dude?" she asked.

"I dig skating, that's all. But I'd dig it even more if me and the guys were out freestyling." He heard Bobby calling to him, and said to Chelsea, "Time for some free grub and drinks on Eddie G. I'm sure there's enough for everybody. How about getting the Shooters together and stopping by? We'll be over by the gate."

"Super," Chelsea smiled. "Catch you later."

Petey wheeled over to where Tom and Bobby were about to leave the ramp.

A few minutes later, the boys were on their second burger and third Coke, when Jordan rolled up. He was so excited that his short, spiky blond hair seemed to stand on end. He was cradling something in his arms and skating even more slowly than usual. "Hey, fellow Wizards!" he yelled. "Check out my birthday present from my folks!"

Jordan came to a gradual stop, grinning proudly. Then he stepped off his board and removed a black canvas cover from what he was carrying.

"Wow!" Petey exclaimed. "Outtasight, dude! A camcorder!"

"Fantastic!" Tom agreed. "Is it really yours?"

"Sure is," Jordan said. "My mom and dad were so psyched about my last report card that they decided to lay this baby on me for my twelfth birthday."

Bobby stared at the minicam, sunlight sparkling on its lens, its black surface clean and professional-looking. "That's really radical. It's about the heaviest birthday present I've ever heard of."

"You can do all kinds of cool things with it," Petey said. "Maybe you'll win ten thousand dollars on *America's Funniest Home Videos*. You could even make videos of us skating and . . ."

Bobby's eyes lit up, and he grabbed Petey by the shoulder. "That's a great idea! We can make a video of our gnarliest, heaviest moves, and then take copies of it around to show dudes who might be interested in sponsoring us!"

"I'm up for it, dudes," Jordan said quickly. "As long as I get to be director."

"It'll be the coolest skating video ever!" Petey roared. "The Street Wizards are gonna have a sponsor!"

2

Petey shot down the sidewalk at top speed, digging the fresh coolness of the morning air. His arms extended, he roared like a jet fighter in a screaming, Mach 2 dive at an enemy target. He cut sharply, sliding the rear of his board, and powered into Bobby's driveway. His Cheap Harold's T-shirt was crisp and new, but his skating shorts were the same grubby, patched, street-worn ones he always wore. When Petey noticed Bobby stepping outside he waved at him. But just then he veered in a different direction—directly toward Jordan and his mini-cam. Jordan scrambled out of the way, abandoning his board. Petey crashed into it broadside and went down on his kneepads, skidding off the concrete past Tom and onto the lawn, still roaring like a jet.

Mrs. Clark, letting out the cat, stood in the doorway smiling at the boys. "I think Petey is here," she said quietly to Bobby. Her smile became even broader and she winked. "But he's such a shy, quiet boy, sometimes it's hard to tell. Jordan, you should make him a star with your wonderful new camera."

"Make me a star?" Petey pretended to be confused. "I thought I already was a star, Mrs. Clark." Bobby' mother laughed and closed the door.

"Star or not," Bobby said, grinning, "it's going to be jammed at Radlands again today. What do you guys think about skating over to the floodway to get in some practice? We'll have room to roll there, and we can lay some grinds on those half-finished curbs."

The other Street Wizards quickly agreed. The huge influx of skaters from all over the West for Megarad was exciting, but getting ramp or pipe time was becoming more and more difficult.

San Carlos was founded during the early days of the computer-chip frenzy and grew rapidly, though many construction projects had lately ground to a halt. The main street, Deacon Blue Boulevard—which the locals called the Main—ran north and south. Intersecting streets ran east and west, creating a gigantic grid. Most of the new houses were modern and many had swimming pools, while the older homes were smaller. Acres of parking lots, used-car dealerships, discount stores, and strip malls surrounded the town.

The floodway was a gigantic government project designed to channel flash-flood water away from the city during the spring runoff. In summertime, it baked in the sun south of town, like the ruins of some ancient civilization that had mysteriously disappeared. The floodway's massive drainpipes, long runs of winding concrete access roads, and stretches of high, sharp-edged curbs were a skater's paradise.

Bobby led the Wizards in a snake line along the sidewalk on the Main. They whooped and whistled as they passed a small bookshop with a sign in its window.

JOIN PARENTS AGAINST SKATEBOARDING
KEEP STREETS OF SAN CARLOS
SAFE AND PEACEFUL

"Those dweebs never give up!" Petey said.

"Maybe we should start Skateboarders Against Parents Against Skateboarding and put signs in windows and stuff," Jordan called out.

"Maybe the P.A.S. will sponsor the Street Wizards!" Tom joked.

The boys kept as close to the curb as possible, leaving pedestrians all the room they needed. The P.A.S. had unsuccessfully tried to outlaw skateboarding in San Carlos. While the group didn't have much to complain about since the San Carlos skaters had gotten rid of a troublemaking gang of thrashers, the Street Wizards and most of the other San Carlos gangs were extra careful when they skated in public places.

16

Petey cut out from the curb toward the center of the sidewalk, eyeing the line of buildings ahead of them. The San Carlos Municipal Center was a big, black-glass-faced structure with a long stairway leading up to the main entrance. The steps were divided by a shiny metal handrail leading from the very top to the sidewalk. It was simply too perfect to pass up. Petey swung out of the snake run and angled up a smooth, low concrete drainage sluice. Before the other guys knew what he was up to, he was at the top, jamming on some speed.

"Lights! Camera! Action!" he shouted to Jordan.

Petey wired a clean olly that put him on top of a raised concrete platform almost level with the handrail. It looked like a mile down to the street, but he wasn't afraid. He pumped once—hard—and tromped on the tail of his board. As he went up he crouched and laid his front trucks over the rail. He swiveled his body slightly, bringing his rear trucks up over the rail as well.

"Power grind comin' at you dudes!" Petey shouted. He shot down the rail toward the sidewalk. Navigating the length of the rail seemed to take less than a second. He hurtled off the end of the rail like a cannonball, put his board into a slide on the sidewalk, and finished the trick by dismounting, kicking down on his board, and grabbing it out of the air as easily as he would catch a ball.

17

"Rad!" Tom exclaimed. "What a power grind!"

"Awesome," Bobby said, almost stunned by the beauty of the trick. "I know you're a heavy grinder, Petey, but that was acute!"

Jordan, his minicam in position, shouted, "I got it! I got it!" He stared up the length of the rail and then shuddered a bit. "Sometimes I think you're nuts, Petey. That was an awesome trick, but it would have scared the pants off of me. I don't like heights."

Petey grinned. "Think something like that's heavy enough to win me a trophy at Megarad?"

Bobby had to hold back what he wanted to say. Petey's stunt was great, but he could very easily have decked a pedestrian when he dismounted, or hurt himself if it had gone badly. Petey was too much of a daredevil sometimes, but Bobby didn't want to bust his chops about it.

"Absolutely, dude," he told Petey. "They might as well give you your cup right now."

"Hey, Petey," Tom called out. "When are you gonna teach me to lay down a grind the way you do?"

"Any time you want," Petey told him. "It's nothing that any skateboarding genius and all-around athlete can't learn in twenty or thirty years!"

When the Street Wizards arrived at the floodway, Jordan skated about slowly, his minicam in position, taping his friends as they ran through their moves. Tom wheeled up next to him. "You're really having a blast with that camera, aren't you?"

Jordan focused on Bobby spiking a long olly. "Yeah," he said, smiling. "I can't skate like you or Bobby, and I don't have the guts Petey has. So you guys lay down the moves and I'll pick them up on tape. OK?"

A few minutes later, Scott Longo and the Pipe Riders wheeled over to where the Wizards were skating. Brad Munson sneered at Petey. "Maybe you dorks ought to go home and skate in your backyards. You don't have enough guts to do any real freestyling!"

"What's that supposed to mean, squidface?" Petey growled. "We're working on our moves for Megarad. Anything wrong with that?"

"You guys are lame," Scott said. "Burn and lots of the other pros are pullin' some radical stuff at a new place we found to skate."

"Burn?" Bobby asked. "Who's Burn? I never heard of the dude."

"You will hear about him, dweeb. Corey Burnhart, the pro sponsored by Digger Sneaks. All his friends call him Burn. He's only the heaviest skater in California—probably heavier than the Lion even." The Lion, Dan Lyons' son, was an internationally respected skateboarder. He was twenty years old and had been touring as a pro for years.

"Yeah," Brad sneered. "If the Lion's father didn't own Radlands, the guy probably wouldn't be able to stay on a board without a seat belt!"

"The Lion was a pro before his dad built Radlands," Bobby answered. "Like Petey said, we're practicing for the competition. If you don't like it, keep rolling."

"What a bunch of geeks," Scott jeered. "If you had any cool, you'd be dicing at the new place—but the Wizards never had any style."

"We can outskate you dorks any day of the week," Petey snarled. "Freestyle, ramp, pipe, anything!"

Scott's face flushed. "Talking isn't skating, Marino. I dare you lamebrains to follow us. We'll show you what skateboarding's all about—if you've got the guts!"

"We've got the guts," Petey said, his features set in a grim expression. "Right, Bobby?"

"Roll, Scott," Bobby said. "We'll follow you and check out this heavy new spot. If it's anything at all, we'll show you some real skating!"

They skated down the access road. The cement reflected the heat upward, and all of the boys were sweating when they came in sight of an immense drainage pipe that emptied into the floodway. A group of skaters—including Penny Ketchum and several other pros—were gathered around the gaping mouth of the concrete pipe, which was twelve feet across. Someone had hauled along a boom box, and classic rock, distorted and amplified inside the pipe, echoed across the cement wasteland.

The Street Wizards stopped and gawked at the enormous drainpipe. "Rad," Petey exclaimed. "How come we didn't find this baby before?"

"It's heavy all right," Tom agreed.

"Wow!" Bobby said. "Look at that dude!" Inside the drainage pipe, one of the pros had gathered speed and was blasting toward the opening. It was the tall blond guy the Wizards had seen the day before at Radlands. The dude's mouth was curled into a sneering smile, and he handled his board as if it were a part of him.

"That's Burn," Scott said. "Scope out how a real pro skates!"

Burn angled upward, cut back down pumping, headed up again—then ran the full circumference of the pipe at killer speed, hanging completely upside down for a few seconds as he followed the curve of the pipe.

"Outtasight," Petey said, almost too quietly for anyone else to hear. He was impressed.

A girl who looked about Corey Burn's age—eighteen or so—skated into the pipe, cheering for him. She road a custom board that reflected light in bright slivers that hurt the eye. Her shirt carried the logo of Zap Wheel Company, along with a pro batch.

"That's Heidi," Scott said. "She's a dynamite skater—and I think she digs me. Heidi, hey Heidi! It's me—Scott Longo—your main dude!" The girl didn't even turn to look at him.

Burn and Heidi joined hands and skated deeper into the pipe. They moved perfectly together, like a pair of professional dancers, laying some speed on the inside of the pipe.

"Ready?" Burn's voice echoed out of the drainage pipe as he called to Heidi.

"Any time you are," Heidi answered.

They ran up high, cut back down, and rocketed up the opposite slope, still clenching each other's hand. They fired around the top of the pipe, then back down the slope. The other skaters yelled and cheered.

As the couple skated out of the pipe, Burn seemed to notice Petey in the crowd. He said something to Heidi, and they skated in the Wizards' direction, ignoring the skaters who tried to talk to them. The couple pulled up in front of the Wizards. Heidi smiled at them, but Corey didn't bother.

"You lay down a decent grind for an amateur," Burn said to Petey. "We were driving by just as you made your run down the rail at the Darth Vader Building downtown."

"Darth Vader Building?" Petey asked. "What are you talking about?"

"Get with it or get left behind, dude—I'm talking about the Municipal Building with all that black glass and the mile of steel railing. Like I said, you put a fair roller coaster on it."

Burn smiled as if he'd given a gift of great value to Petey. "Keep it up and one day you might be about half as heavy as I am on street moves, kid," he continued. "For a dude who only has this crummy little town and that lame Radlands place to skate, you show some style."

Heidi blushed a bit at Corey's bragging. "You looked great," she said, smiling at Petey. "It was a radical grind."

Corey Burnhart looked at the drainage pipe and back at Petey. "Hang in there." He skated off with Heidi a board's length behind him.

"What a flying dork that dude is," Bobby said.

"If he doesn't like San Carlos or Radlands," Tom said, "I'd be happy to show him the road leading out of town."

Jordan was also bugged by the pro's attitude. "I guess a guy like him doesn't need friends—nobody could like him anywhere near as much as he likes himself."

Petey opened his mouth to say something when a commotion by the drainage pipe caught their attention.

"I'm next!" Penny shouted, moving to the mouth of the pipe.

"No, you're not!" yelled a dude wearing a pro shirt from Acme Skateboard Company, in L.A. "I want a shot at that baby!"

"You're both wrong," a skater in a *Thrasher* magazine T-shirt hollered. "I'm hittin' it right now!"

Petey hurried to join the skaters at the mouth of the pipe.

"Are you clowns all nuts?" a voice rang out over the blaring music and the skateboarders' shouts. The Lion skidded to a halt on the roadway and stood glaring at the group, his hands on his hips.

He shook his head as he eyed Burn and Heidi. "Ever heard of helmets?" the Lion snapped sarcastically. "They're real popular here in San Carlos. And somebody's going to get wrecked running verts inside that pipe," he added.

"Aw, pack it, man," Burn answered. "If you're afraid of the place, split and leave the rest of us alone!"

The Lion glared at him for a moment, then looked at the others. "Scott, Bobby, Brad, Chelsea, Tom, Jordan, Petey! This is crazy. Somebody's going to get creamed here. Look at the height of that thing—it'd be like falling out of a second-story window!"

"That's what makes it so heavy . . ." Petey began.

"Chill, Marino!" the Lion snapped. "I like a challenge more than any of you dudes do—the tougher the better. But what's going to happen to skateboarding in San Carlos if the P.A.S. hears about what's going on here? Why don't you think about that!"

"He's right," Bobby told the other Wizards.

Chelsea agreed. "The Lion is, like, making sense," she told her girls, the Shooters. "We don't have to end up as grease spots on this pipe to show we can skate. Let's hit Radlands. It probably won't be so crowded, 'cause like, everybody's here."

"Don't listen to those dorks," Scott told the Pipe Riders, keeping his voice low so the Lion wouldn't hear him. "The Lion can't tell us how to skate or where to skate. Right, Burn?"

"Dig it," Burn said, loudly enough for everyone to hear. "I skate where I want and how I want. I'm not some dweeb who's scared off because somethin' might be a little dangerous. That makes it even more of a rush."

"Come on, you guys," Bobby said. "Let's go back where we were and run some more of our routines. There's nothing for the Street Wizards here." Tom and Jordan were standing right in front of Bobby. He looked around for Petey.

Petey stood on the deck of his board, looking into the dark mouth of the awesome drainage pipe. The boom box was still blaring—the Doors playing "Light My Fire." He stared at the top of the pipe, imagining the incredible sensation of making a complete loop of it on his board and hanging upside down for a fraction of a second—or longer.

Bobby rolled up next to him. "We're going to go back. Come on, Petey—you know the Lion's right. This is too dangerous. Why risk getting busted up?"

For a long moment Petey didn't take his eyes off the pipe. "If the Lion hadn't showed up, I could have hung a really acute vert."

"That's not the point," Bobby said. "You probably could. But it's crazy. You could get wasted trying to spike a heavy stunt like that."

Petey shrugged. "So? Maybe freestyling's just a little more dangerous than rampin'. I don't go trying to wreck your fun when you guys are pulling moves, do I?"

Tom and Jordan skated over.

"What's up?" Tom asked.

"Nothing," Bobby answered quickly. "We're ready to go back and do some skating, right, Petey? Hey, let's stop by my place for something to drink."

Petey took a final look at the pipe. "Yeah," he finally answered, "I guess so."

The Shooters collected around the Lion, chatting and laughing as they skated away from the pipe. Most of the pros followed, including Penny. Scott and the Pipe Riders hung back, grumbling to one another, until Corey Burnhart and Heidi gave them a signal, and they skated off, up the floodway.

Petey skated to the end of the Wizards' snake line, and didn't say another word on the way back to Bobby's house.

3

"Roll, dudes! I'm ready to catch anything heavy on tape. C'mon, give me some radical footage for our demo!"

An early-morning breeze whipped the Megarad banner flying over Radlands' Ramp 2. Jordan, on the platform above the ramp, fiddled with the adjustments on his camcorder, checking exposure and glare through the eyepiece. The brilliant California sun made a filter necessary almost all the time.

Bobby grinned at Tom as they rolled slowly along the valley of the ramp. "He's really into it, isn't he?"

"Sure is," Tom answered. "He thinks he's the next Steven Spielberg."

"Bobby," Jordan yelled, "put on some power! Let's see some flash!"

Bobby shoved hard with his foot and rode up the slope a few feet. When he reversed and shot back down he pumped a couple of times for speed, all the while smiling to himself. The sound of his wheels, the feel of the deck under his skating sneaks, the breeze in his face—it was all awesome. He had good momentum after another run up and down the slope, and he used the speed to blast up toward the coping at the top of the ramp. He crouched down about halfway, his left hand falling perfectly into place on the grip tape on the edge of his board.

The coping seemed to be charging at him. He lowered his crouch a hair and shifted his left foot a few millimeters for ideal balance. Then he was past the coping, blasting into the inky blue sky, grabbing a ton of air. His right hand shot downward like a snake striking, and he locked a grip on the coping, holding his board against his soles with his other hand. The power of his run carried his body upward, and he hung in midair, balanced on his arm, for as long as he dared, tweaking the move for everything it was worth. As he dropped back to the ramp, his board touched down squarely and smoothly. He ran down the slope and cut hard in the valley; he knew he'd spiked a difficult trick.

"Fantastic!" Jordan hollered, his voice almost quivering with excitement. "And I caught every second of that handplant! Outtasight, dude!"

"Tough move, Bobby," Tom said. "You looked

like a real pro on that one." He skated up next to his friend. "Ready to try out the trick we talked about earlier?"

"Let's do it, buddy," Bobby said, still feeling the adrenaline coursing through his veins. "High and fast, right?"

"That's the only way to go," Tom answered, just as psyched as Bobby. "Watch this, Jordan. We've got a little surprise for you and your minicam."

The two boys split up, each heading for one end of the ramp. They piled up speed and momentum by snaking on the slopes and pumping hard in the valley. Their eyes met across several feet of ramp, and they both nodded. They were ready.

Separated by six feet or so, both boys cut straight up, rolling hard. Bobby edged his board slightly to his left. Tom edged his to the right. As they hurtled toward the coping, Tom dropped into a full crouch, keeping his compressed body as close to the deck as he could get it. Bobby rode tall, his knees only slightly bent. Both skaters launched upward at the same time, and their paths crossed in midair. Bobby soared high over Tom, who was still maintaining his tight crouch. Both shouted ecstatically as they touched down. They gave each other high fives as they wheeled into the valley.

"Perfect!" Bobby exclaimed.

"Outtasight!" Tom hollered.

"Dynamite!" Jordan stepped up to the edge of the platform, looking down into the ramp. "OK, dudes," he called out calmly. "I'm ready now. Let's see some action!"

Tom and Bobby were stunned. They stared blankly at one another, their mouths open with disbelief—Jordan had missed the trick!

Jordan couldn't hold back his laughter a second longer. "Don't worry, guys, just joking. I've got it on tape."

"You would have been wearing that camcorder instead of using it if you'd missed that trick," Tom roared with mock sternness.

"What trick?" Petey asked from the platform behind Jordan. He had just arrived.

"If you're on time tomorrow, dude, maybe I'll give you a repeat performance," Bobby said. "Now how about doing some skating before the crowds hit the pipes?"

Petey didn't have to be asked twice. He dropped into the half-pipe and rocketed downward in his favorite position, his arms at his sides like the wings of a diving jet fighter. "Make sure you tape this," he yelled to Jordan. "This move's going to win us a sponsor."

Petey cranked his board around halfway up the ramp and pointed it straight at the valley. He dropped into a quick crouch, his hands clutching the lip of his board on either side. He shoved hard with his arms, kicked his legs up over his head— and crashed and burned like a fresh cut out on a brand-new board.

All the Wizards laughed as Petey skidded down the ramp on his kneepads, clasping his hands over his head as if he had just spiked a radical move. Petey's laughter was just as loud as his friends'.

"Nice skating, dude," Jordan shouted. "I'm gonna send the tape to *America's Funniest Home Videos*."

Petey waved to Jordan with a broad smile, but the smile quickly faded. Pipe Riders Scott Longo, Brad Munson, and Eddie Tedesco appeared on the platform behind Jordan.

"Wearing out your kneepads again, squid?" Brad asked. "You spend most of your time on the pavement, Marino."

"And from the looks of your gut, you spend most of your time at the snack bar!" Petey answered. "Let me ask you something. Have you figured out how to run a piece of flat sidewalk without eating cement yet?"

Brad's face turned bright red. Petey's words made Eddie and Scott laugh, and Brad grew even angrier. "You're a dork, Marino," he snarled. "Keep your yap shut or I'll shut it for you!"

Still in the valley of the ramp, Petey stepped off his board. "Any time, lamebrain. I've listened to your big mouth for too long. Come on down here and . . ."

"Chill, dude," Bobby said sharply. "Punching holes in Munson won't do anything but cause trouble."

Petey wrestled with his temper for a moment before nodding at Bobby. "You're right. I shouldn't let a dweeb like him bug me. I'll go over to Penny's table and grab us some of those free Cokes."

Bobby, Tom, and Jordan heaved a sigh of relief in unison. Petey's temper could be a problem at times, but they all agreed Munson's mouth got old awfully quickly.

Petey skated away from the ramp, using his excess energy to shove his foot against the smooth concrete again and again, building up good speed. Instead of heading for Penny's table, he veered off toward Ramp 2. It was a smaller ramp than 4, and not too many of the skaters were wild about it. Petey had seen the Lion heading out to it earlier. He figured he might as well scope out what the champ was doing. And he didn't want to be around Brad, at least for a little while.

It was still early. The regulars hadn't shown up yet. The pros were around, but they were talking and joking with each other over by the pro shop.

As Petey rolled up to Ramp 2, he heard Mr. Lyons talking to his son. He didn't sound happy.

"That was sloppy, Dave! You could have stopped to have lunch in the time it took you to do that reverse! You better get into it, boy, if you want to do me and your hometown proud at the tournament in Japan."

Petey stepped off his board and carried it the last few yards to the ramp. Neither Mr. Lyons nor the Lion had seen him, and that's the way he wanted it to stay. He couldn't help being curious about what was going on. He watched as the Lion powered up the slope and punched a handplant at the top. It looked pretty good to Petey, but it wasn't anywhere near good enough for Mr. Lyons.

"What's the matter?" he said. "You're skating like an amateur."

"My amateur days are long gone," the Lion snapped at his dad. "But at least back then I didn't have you riding me all the time!"

"I don't ride you all the time," Mr. Lyons said. "It's just that you're the best, so I expect a lot out of you. I built this whole skate park for you. Now here's your chance to do something for me."

"What am I?" the Lion asked sarcastically. "Free publicity?"

"Is a little free publicity too much to ask for?"

Petey stayed in the background as the Lion stepped off his board and, tucking it under his arm, started to walk off the ramp. "The day the Lion's moves come down to publicity stunts," he said calmly to his father, "is the day I stop skating."

Petey didn't wait to hear Mr. Lyon's response. He skated away from Ramp 2 feeling really strange. He'd always thought the Lion and his dad had the world by the ears—one the owner of a gnarly boarding park, and the other a skater who had won tournaments all over the world. Petey stopped and sat down on his board, his back against the tall fence that surrounded the park. The relative quiet was a relief.

Petey picked at the CHEAP HAROLD'S lettering on his shirt. *Maybe there's too much stuff like this,* he thought. *Free shirts and hot dogs and Cokes—for what? To hype some dude's board store, or some kind of sneakers, that's what.* He sighed, stood up, and climbed onto the deck of his board.

As he skated toward the gate, Petey didn't feel like going right back to the other Wizards. They were still his best friends, of course, but something was bothering him, and he couldn't put his finger on it. The fact that he dug street freestyling while the rest of the Wizards were hot on ramp stuff made him feel left out of the gang.

A fresh cut Petey had seen a couple of times rolled up next to him. Petey nodded at the dude, then said, "Sometimes I wish skating could be as fun as it used to be, without all this Megarad hype and jive."

"I think it's fun having the competition here," the new skater said. "And the more I can learn about ramping, the sooner I'll have a big-bucks sponsor, know what I mean?"

Petey shook his head and wheeled away from the dude without answering. He shot through Radlands' front gate, then suddenly dragged his board to a grinding stop. A shiny black van was parked on the street ten yards away. Two oversized video cameras were mounted in harnesses on its roof, each with an operator. In the parking lot, at least a dozen dudes in flashy clothes were hustling around holding light meters and shouting at each other.

Two guys who looked as if they had twice as many teeth as ordinary humans were walking around with microphones in their hands and sound packs clipped to their lizard-skin belts. Several girls in slinky dresses followed right behind these geeks.

Petey stood there holding his board, watching all the action, trying to figure out what was happening. He looked over at the van again. Lettered on the side in red was CABLE NEWS NETWORK 7. A dork whose hair seemed enameled into place looked up at one of the cameramen and said something Petey couldn't make out. When the cameraman turned to answer, Petey noticed, on the back of his jacket, the Cable 7 logo and, under that, the words THE WORLD OF SKATEBOARDING.

"Man!" Petey exclaimed. He'd seen the show. These people weren't playing games—this was a real-live film crew!

4

Petey couldn't take his eyes off the frenzied action around him. Suddenly, one of the guys with a microphone came over to him.

"Howdy, young dude!" he said through a bright, toothy smile. "You look like a real skateboarder to me. Want to answer a few questions for *The World of Skateboarding*? I'm Mike McGee, the baddest emcee, and I come straight at you every week on Cable 7!"

"I ... uh ..." Petey stuttered, wondering how anybody would pay a lame geek like this to do anything.

"Don't let my stardom freeze up your head, little dude," Mike McGee rattled on. "Just talk to me the way you talk to the other dudes and dudettes at Radlands."

"Dudettes?" Petey asked, not sure if the guy was serious.

"Hey, I'll tell you this, little buddy. I know the

lingo you skaters use. That's why I'm the world's baddest emcee. I don't just walk the walk, I talk the talk. Can you dig it?"

"I . . . well, I . . ." Petey mumbled again. He took a step back. The man's mike was almost jammed against Petey's chin. And he smelled as if he'd fallen into a vat of cheap after-shave.

"You got a handle, little dude? Come on, talk to my millions of fans."

"Handle? I . . . uhh . . ."

"Your name, boy! Get with it! No reason to be awed by me. I'm just your average home-grown TV star. Dig it?"

"I'm . . . Petey Marino."

"Petey! Heavy name! Petey Maroni—great to meet you, dude! Tell me, Petey, who's the biggest, baddest skater at Radlands?"

"Well . . ." Petey said, shifting his weight from foot to foot. He looked around, trying to find a path he could bolt over to get away from this flying squid. "Bobby Clark's pretty heavy, and there are . . ."

"You mean it's a toss-up between Corey Burnhart and Dave Lyons, right?" Mike McGee asked. Although his smile was still a yard wide, his eyes said that Petey better give him the answer he wanted.

Petey suddenly felt much more comfortable. He

looked at the camera operators on top of the van and waved. "Hi Mom, hi Dad!" he shouted.

Mike McGee forced a smile. "Always nice to come across a dude who really digs his folks. What does your dad do for a living?"

Petey couldn't help himself. "Well, he's an ax-murderer, Mike. I'm glad—really glad—you asked. And my mom's a dudette. It doesn't pay much, but she loves to skate. I've got a brother who drills holes in cabbages and then sells them as bowling balls." Just then, Petey saw the other Street Wizards skating toward him. He looked at Mike McGee. "I'd like to say hello to some of my friends . . ."

Mike McGee made a cut motion across his throat to stop the cameras. "You little creep," he snarled, no longer smiling. "You could have been on national TV."

Petey dropped his board, climbed on, and pushed off. "Yeah," he shouted over his shoulder. "And you could have had a life if you weren't such a dork!"

The other Wizards were almost paralyzed with laughter. Bobby was bent over at the waist. Tom fell off his board and rolled on the hot parking-lot pavement. Jordan had carefully set his minicam on the deck of his board before he collapsed next to it, laughing so hard tears appeared in his eyes.

Petey skidded to a stop alongside his pals. "Did you hear that turkey?"

But the humor was lost on everyone except the Street Wizards. Word that Mike McGee, from *The World of Skateboarding*, was in town had spread like wildfire. The Pipe Riders wheeled by, scorching to grab a couple of seconds on TV. Even Chelsea McIntyre and the Shooters rolled hard toward the black van, one of the girls running a comb through her hair as she skated.

The camera team was moving into the park. Skaters crashed into each other trying to catch Mike McGee's eye. Scott Longo, smiling like a true dweeb, cut sharply toward the broadcaster and attempted a sliding stop. Unfortunately, two other dudes were heading in that direction at the same time. All three came together in a twisted mess of arms, legs, and skateboards. Then Corey Burnhart and Heidi skated up, followed closely by a bunch of their groupies.

Burnhart tried to slide up next to McGee, but one of the baddest emcee's flunkies stepped in front of his skateboard.

"Hey," Corey said loudly, "me and Mike are buddies! Let me through!"

Mike McGee glanced over at Burnhart for half a second, then looked away. "Tell that kid I don't need another interview with him right now," he instructed one of his crew. "I'll let him know when I do—if I do."

The Street Wizards were weak from laughter as

they watched the other skaters' lame efforts to be noticed by the TV crew. Every few minutes there would be another crash of kids jockeying for position in front of the cameras, and the Wizards would crack up all over again.

Petey watched the surging crowd ebb and flow. "I've never seen Radlands this crowded. How about splitting from here and doin' some freestyling at some of our old favorite places? All this TV junk is a royal pain."

Bobby nodded. "Sounds good to me. We can lay down some grinds and maybe play a little board tag."

"And I'll keep on taping," Jordan said. "I've got some real heavy stuff. I caught all your aggro tricks, but I've been shooting you guys on the sly, too. Some of that candid footage will look good to a sponsor. You know, relaxing on your boards and that type of stuff."

"What are we waiting for?" Tom asked.

The Street Wizards skated through the parking lots of the stores and drive-ins along the Main, until they were close to San Carlos's downtown core. Some of the streets there had been blocked off to traffic and turned into pedestrian malls. But there were never any pedestrians, because in California everyone drove.

"I've had enough snakin' for now!" Petey yelled,

powering out of line and careening into the empty street. "It's time to see if my trucks can take some more rad abuse!"

They were on a short block of flower shops, old bookstores, and pastry shops. Petey scribed an arc back to the curb rolling flat out. At the last millisecond before impact he stomped the tail of his board and laid his front trucks on the curb, grinding along for a good dozen feet before he croaked the move, wheeled out into the street, and ollied up onto the sidewalk. The others had slowed to watch his freestyling, and cheered when he was finished.

Petey dragged his board around in a skidding 360. He was balanced perfectly, his arms loose and his hands tucked casually into his pockets. He stepped off his board and bowed deeply, a mile-wide grin plastered on his face. "Dig it, dudes!" he shouted to his pals. "This is what skateboarding is all about."

Bobby and Tom peeled off and raced along the razor's edge of the curb, the nose of Tom's board almost kissing the tail of Bobby's.

"Hit it!" Tom shouted.

Bobby tromped down with his left foot and set his trucks on the edge at the same time as Tom. Together they put an acute grind on the curb that brought a cheer from Petey. Jordan aimed his minicam, panning like a professional camera operator to capture the fast action.

The Street Wizards swooped around the building on the corner, keeping tight to the curb, riding the sidewalk. Petey spiked an olly that carried him high and hard over a grate, and Bobby and Tom each aped the move, Bobby pulling the same awesome distance and height, Tom's trick only a little shorter and lower.

Petey jammed down the tail of his board and slid to a stop. He stared across the street at a building that brought a slow, spreading smile to his face. Bobby wheeled back and followed Petey's eyes, as did Jordan and Tom.

"Unbelievable," Petey whispered with reverence, looking up. "Last time I was on this street, this place wasn't even half-finished."

Across the street stood San Carlos Senior Citizens Center, its many windows reflecting the strong sunlight. But Petey was interested less in the building than in the walkway that led from the street to the front doors. A series of wide, low concrete steps ran from the sidewalk halfway to the doors, then angled in the opposite direction, still going upward. Running down the center of the steps was a three-foot high cement wall, on top of which was a polished metal handrail.

"Awesome," Bobby agreed. "But you're not thinking . . ."

"I sure am!" Petey yelled over his shoulder, dashing across the street with his board clutched in his right hand. He took the steps to the front doors of the Senior Center two at a time. At the top he looked around, surveying the territory as if it belonged to him. He saw hardly anyone, and only a few cars crawled up and down the quiet street. An old gent walking a collie on the sidewalk walked past without paying any attention to him. A hand-holding couple were interested more in each other than in some kid with a skateboard. Otherwise, the immediate vicinity was free of traffic.

"Bobby!" Jordan exclaimed. "You've got to stop him! He'll break his neck!"

Tom was worried too, nibbling on his lower lip as he eyed the long rail. "What about the kink there where the rail changes direction and goes on up?" he asked. "Maybe we better try to talk him out of it."

"Not this time," Bobby decided. "Remember that run he spiked at the Municipal Building? Petey can handle this. At least I'm pretty sure he can." He smiled. "Even if he can't, he's going to run it, and the only way we could stop him would be to tie him up and sit on him, right?"

Tom shook his head. "I don't know about this. It would take a real heavy freestyler to spike a run on that rail."

"That's my point," Bobby said. "Maybe we

haven't been watching Petey's skating close enough because he's such a flaming nut case all the time. We should start paying more attention."

Jordan positioned himself to the side of the steps, his minicam slowly sweeping the entire length of the rail and then focusing on Petey, standing at the top.

The cement wall extended a few inches on either side. Petey looked around. There was nothing nearby to olly from, so that he could land on the form, and there was no way to get up enough speed to olly to it from the ground. Simply setting his board on the rail seemed like a fresh-cut move, but there didn't seem to be any other option. Unless . . .

Petey sauntered up to the doors of the Senior Center and peeked in through the glass. There was a reception desk, but no one was sitting behind it. Two beige vinyl sofas faced each other in the lobby, but they were empty. He pushed open one of the doors, digging the air-conditioned cool that washed over him. Quickly he bent down and flipped the little lever to hold the door open. The sill was a slab of marble raised only an inch or so, designed to accommodate people with a cane or a walker, or in a wheelchair.

He walked up to the desk, took another quick look around, and dropped his board onto the polished floor. A heartbeat later he shot through the doorway, tromped the tail of his board, and flew at the rail. His front truck nicked home and the rear one followed. Suddenly he was riding the longest and fastest roller coaster of his life. He heard the sweet sound of aluminum rasping against metal.

Petey crouched on his board, his arms slightly away from his body, his face a mask of concentration combined with sheer joy. The kink hurtled toward him, but he was ready for it. He dropped all his weight onto the tail of his board, hiking the nose. Then, at the crucial moment, he shifted his weight and swung his knees sharply to the side. The nose of his board flicked into line with the rail once again, and his trucks kissed down a millisecond later. He rode the rail to the sidewalk standing almost straight up. He rocketed off the trail and touched down with a jarring bang that felt as if it would pop the fillings out of his teeth. His board rolled to a stop on its own.

Bobby and Tom rushed at him, their faces bright with amazement.

"Awesome!" Tom roared.

"Megarad!" Bobby whacked Petey on the shoulder, laughing crazily. "Acute power grind, Petey!"

Jordan was almost as excited as Petey. "I got it all," he yelled. Patting his minicam, he told them, "I got every inch of the heaviest roller coaster any dude ever pulled, right here in living color!"

5

"But Petey," Bobby explained again as the boys rolled through the streets in the general direction of Radlands, "we've got to get our ramp moves down for the competition."

"I didn't say the Wizards don't need to practice." Petey pushed down sharply with his foot, rolling up next to Bobby. "All I said is that I'm getting tired of fighting crowds of dudes with pro shirts on. What fun is waiting in line to run a grind?"

"I say we forget Radlands for the day and have some fun instead!" Petey said, loudly enough for Tom and Jordan to hear as well.

Bobby thought for a moment, holding back the anger he was starting to feel. "Let's see what the other guys think."

Petey wasn't ready to back down. "OK. But I'll tell you right now—I'm not crowd skating today, no matter what you dudes decide."

Tom and Jordan exchanged worried looks.

48

"Maybe we could use some time away from the ramps. We haven't hit the back lot of the K-mart lately," Tom pointed out. "It's an awesome place for practicing freestyle."

No one had any problems with the idea.

"Let's roll, then!" Petey shouted with a somewhat forced burst of enthusiasm. He noticed that Bobby's jaw was set tightly as he skated along. Petey thought about making some kind of joke to ease the tension, then decided against it.

"I'm not going to apologize for wanting to do some street skating," he grumbled softly. "Not to anyone!"

"What?" Bobby asked, glaring at Petey.

"I . . . nothing. Forget it."

The snake run took them through San Carlos, across the Main, and then alongside a wide, busy freeway that ran past a gigantic K-mart. The Street Wizards waited on the shoulder, their boards in hand. The gang had a hard rule about the freeway and skateboards—the two didn't mix. They also had a hard rule about safety gear: No Street Wizard ever skated without a helmet, kneepads, and elbowpads, no matter how short a run he was making.

The K-mart parking lot was jammed with cars and pedestrians, and the boys skated down its long, sloping side, past the store, and through an access alley to the smaller parking lot in the rear. On the two-and-a-half-acre concrete lot there were only a few cars and a pair of huge dumpsters.

"How about an obstacle course?" Tom suggested. "We can set up a real hairy one, and maybe Jordan can grab some radical turning shots and ollies for our tape."

The boys scrounged around behind the store and in the adjacent field, hauling obstacles back to the lot. Tom found a few empty paint cans some jerk had dumped in the field, and from a ditch Bobby dragged a half-crushed metal drum, which he set up as a jump.

Petey scored a pair of crumbling cinder blocks. He placed them a couple of feet apart and laid a dead tree limb on top, creating another jump. Jordan set down fist-sized rocks every few feet to delineate the course, building in lots of curves and a couple of right-angle turns as well. The boys skated the course slowly, in a line, to get the feel of it.

"Jordan, you take first whack at it," Petey said. "Let's see you scorch the course, dude!"

"Burn it!" Tom shouted.

"Yeah," Bobby added, holding the camcorder, which Jordan had taught him to operate. "Hit it, Jordan! Give me something to shoot at."

All the voices sounded kind of strained to Petey—even his own. It was as if other Wizards were doing something against their will, just to make him happy. Petey skated a couple of yards away from Tom and Bobby to watch Jordan run the course. Neither of the boys followed Petey.

For a slightly chubby kid who wasn't a natural athlete, Jordan did a good job. He blew Petey's jump, but pulled a shaky olly that carried him over Bobby's barrel. He cut nicely around the paint cans, and handled the right angles and the curves like a thrasher. He was grinning and breathing hard when he finished the run and took back the camcorder from Bobby. Jordan was ready to go back to being a director.

Petey was setting up for a run when girls' voices and the hum of skateboard wheels caught the gang's attention. Chelsea McIntyre rolled onto the lot from the access alley, her long blond hair trailing behind her in the breeze. The rest of the Shooters followed her as she wheeled up to the obstacle course.

Petey heaved a sigh of relief when he saw the girls, figuring they'd help break the tension. He covered his eyes, pretending to be in pain. "That hot pink you guys wear burns my eyes!"

Chelsea waved at him. "It'd have to burn your eyes, 'cause your mind's been burned out for years!"

The Shooters dragged their hot-pink boards to sliding stops.

"Have you dudes heard about the Graffiti Run?"

Chelsea asked excitedly. "Corey Burnhart—the guy they call Burn—is putting it on. There's going to be free Cokes and snacks and stuff, and we can all spray-paint anything we want to on this huge wall."

"Yeah, right," Bobby said doubtfully. "And end up having the San Carlos cops call our folks and tell them about it."

"No," Chelsea said. "It's the big wall around the parking lot of that supermarket that went out of business on the Main. Some dude is putting a computer-and-video store in there. Burn said the wall's gonna be torn down anyway, so the new owner doesn't mind what we do to it. Digger Sneaks is laying out the bread for the snacks."

"Free snacks?" Petey asked. "I can dig that. And doin' some legal spray-painting will be acute."

"Who's bringing the spray paint?" Jordan asked. "That stuff is expensive—I buy it for my rocket models."

"Digger Sneaks is," explained Mandy, a red-headed Shooter. "And they even hired a dude named Eugene something, from L.A., who's this big graffiti artist."

"We're going over after we buy some tapes in here," Chelsea said, pointing to the back wall of the K-mart. "Are you dudes gonna make it? Could be a rad time."

Bobby looked at his fellow Wizards, who all nodded. "Sure," he answered for the gang. "Want us to wait for you?"

"Awesome! We can all skate over together," Chelsea said. "We'll be out in five minutes, OK?"

The Street Wizards tugged their obstacles back to where they had found them and skated to the front of the store. Half an hour later, Petey remarked, "Longest five minutes I ever spent." Fifteen minutes after that the Shooters came out of the K-mart clutching shopping bags, and the two gangs set out for the Main.

The Graffiti Run wall was eight feet high and made of concrete blocks that had been painted a dull gray some time ago. The lot it enclosed looked very small because of the number of skateboarders milling around it. The graffiti artist had been at work for a few hours creating what looked like a page from a gigantic coloring book on the wall. He'd painted only outlines of skating scenes and skaters, and it was up to the San Carlos boarders to fill in the shapes and forms with the wild colors provided by Digger Sneaks.

Corey stood against the wall, exactly halfway from one end to the other. Behind him was a massive fluorescent-red painting of a heart with a pair of sneaks in the center. Across the heart in eye-shattering green was the name BURNHART and the slogan A NEW KIND OF SHOE FOR TODAY! Under that was the Digger Sneaks logo.

The pro was in his glory, passing out soft drinks, cans of spray paint, and sneaker-shaped cookies. A group of girls hung close to him, not bothering to produce any graffiti, and he was digging them. Heidi skated brusquely in and out of the bunch of groupies, cutting close to them without saying a word. Music blared across the lot. Skaters were spiking ollies and laying down other tricks in what few bits of open pavement they could find. It was a giant party, and everybody was having a good time.

Jordan noticed the tape in his camcorder was almost full, and decided to get a replacement. He walked into the video-and-computer store, whose owner was preparing for the grand opening.

"Nice camcorder," the guy said, smiling at Jordan. "If you had waited and bought it here, I could have saved you some green."

"Birthday present from my folks," Jordan said. "I don't know where they bought it." He looked around the store, which was packed with computers, TVs, video cameras, and other electronic equipment. "Boy, lots of heavy stuff. You'll make a mint here."

"I'm counting on it. My wife and I are new to San Carlos, and we've mortgaged everything but our teeth to get this place up and running." He paused for a moment, looking at Jordan. "Say, you must be a native here. Tell me something. What do I have to do to get word about my store around? I can't afford press or TV, and even radio time's steep."

Jordan smiled as a brainstorm almost swept him off his feet. "What I'd do is sponsor some skateboarders—maybe a gang," he said carefully. "They'd skate around town with your name on their shirts, and anywhere they went, they'd talk up your store. Lots of companies do it—like Digger Sneaks out there."

The store owner nodded slowly. "Never thought of that. I used to do quite a bit of 'boarding when I was younger. I used to skate with a gang called the Pool Rats, over near Fresno." He paused, smiling. "We were pretty heavy into concrete pools—empty ones. Some of them we even had permission to skate in," he said, and laughed. "You know, your idea is good. But I don't know the kids or the gangs around here. How would I know I'm sponsoring top guns? I don't have the time to scout skateboarders."

"Simple." Jordan grinned. "You watch a video of the gang. If their skating turns you on, you sign them up and pay for their touring and some of their gear. If you're not impressed, you don't sign them and nobody loses anything."

"You mean these kids have videos of their tricks?"

"Not all of them. But the Street Wizards do," Jordan told him. "Or they will real soon. I'm a member, and we're putting together some real hot scenes."

The man grinned and held out his hand. "My name's Don Trumble. And I'm not making any promises, but bring that video over to me the minute it's finished and I'll have a look. Then, well, we'll see what happens. OK?"

"Great!" Jordan exclaimed. "You won't be disappointed, Mr. Trumble. I guarantee that!"

When Jordan bolted out of the store to share his news with the Street Wizards, he found himself in the middle of a paint riot—kids were painting the wall, the parking lot, and each other. Corey Burnhart charged by on his board, clutching a can of spray paint in his hand. "Nobody paints me and gets away with it!" he yelled.

Jordan noticed a wide swatch of bright red across the pro's T-shirt.

Heidi raced through the crowd on her board, red paint splattered all over her hands and arms. Still holding the can of red paint in one hand, she shouted over her shoulder as she fled, "Maybe not—but I just did!"

Some of the Shooters were digging the painting action, laughing and screaming as they sprayed the wall and any skater who rolled by. A redhead who had good moves and handled her board well cut sharply around Jordan, aimed her can, but lowered it when she saw the camcorder.

"You got lucky, dude!" she shrieked. A pro from Boardmaster's Wheels and Supplies didn't do as well. In a flash the redhead sprayed a fat Z on the front of his T-shirt.

Brad zipped out of the crowd, a can of paint in either hand, grinning like a kid on Christmas morning. "I really dig art!" he roared as he painted a couple of fresh cuts who were slow to get rolling out of his path.

Jordan skirted the painting scene, looking for the Wizards. He saw Tom and Bobby standing with a bunch of kids at one end of the parking lot, all facing away from him. They were obviously watching something, and Jordan didn't have to guess what it was. That many board crazies could be scoping only one thing—a rad skater cranking on some acute moves. He hustled over to a spot just behind Corey Burnhart and Heidi, both of whom had given up squabbling to check out skating.

When Jordan got there Petey was dicing with Scott, Chelsea, and a couple of boarders from other gangs. The skaters were rolling hard, spiking one freestyle trick after another.

Scott smacked a fast, tight grind on one of the rounded lengths of cement that had been placed to keep cars from banging their front ends into the wall. "Top that, Marino!" he shouted, grinning at Burnhart and Heidi.

Petey cut a figure eight, pumping like crazy and

putting on speed. He fired at the length of cement Scott had just burned, approaching it in warp drive. He kicked his nose up without losing momentum, and kissed his trucks down perfectly. The grind was awesome. Petey was in radical form.

The crowd gasped as he burned over the first cement length. He let his speed carry him to the next one, a couple of feet away. He laid down another grind that carried him half the length of the second one. Chelsea skidded in a 360 and saluted Petey with a clenched fist. He swept his board off the form, shoved with his foot a couple of times to get rolling again, and cranked out a long olly, which he croaked by stamping down on the nose of his board. Then he spun in a full 360, his board grinding noisily on the flat pavement. The audience gasped again, and some of them—led by Bobby, Tom, and Jordan—clapped and whooped.

Scott swallowed hard and shoved off again, grunting with the effort as he gathered speed. He punched a frontside turn and added a fakie that had some cool on it, especially when he added a sliding 180. Petey was even hotter now. He missed nicking Scott's board by a couple of millimeters. Scott bailed out, then just stood there, flushing bright red and feeling foolish because he'd scrubbed his run for nothing.

Petey cut a sharp right turn, crouching low on his deck, leaning back to raise the nose of his board.

He got it up high, then higher, lifting it until he almost went over backward. Then he dropped down hard and swung into a grinding left. He stood and pumped hard, gaining power to lay another grind on one of the cement lengths near the wall.

He lifted off the grind while he was still moving fast and edged into a 180 that was smooth and effortless. Then, a fraction of a second before his board stopped completely, Petey stepped off the deck, stomped the nose, and grabbed his board out of the air by its lip. His face was covered with sweat, and he sucked air hungrily.

"Awesome!" Heidi shrieked.

Corey Burnhart lost his ultra-cool for a moment and yelled along with Heidi. "Radical! Super-rad!"

Petey rolled over to the Street Wizards as other freestyle honchos moved into the open area. He smiled broadly at Scott, who scowled and turned to his Pipe Rider buddies.

Petey grabbed the Coke Bobby held out to him and drained the bottle in three long, noisy swallows. Scott was glaring at him again. This time, Petey winked at him.

Tom, Bobby, and Jordan huddled around Petey. Petey, still sucking air into his starving lungs, couldn't talk yet—but there was really nothing to say. He hadn't missed Corey's and Heidi's cheers, but the pride the Street Wizards felt in him was far more important. Tom slapped him on his back, going on and on about the acute moves. Bobby joined in, cheering and laughing. Petey threw an arm over each of their shoulders, grinning at Jordan.

"Did you get it all?" he asked.

Jordan's smile disappeared. "I . . . I wasn't taping. I was just in the computer store and the owner said he might sponsor us, and I guess I forgot why I went in there in the first place. I hustled over to tell you dudes. I'm really sorry, Petey, I just didn't have enough tape to catch your move. Just wait, the next time you . . ."

"Sponsor us?" Tom blurted out. "Really?"

"What did he say?" Bobby asked, moving toward Jordan.

Petey ran the back of his hand across his sweaty forehead. His smile was also gone. "You wouldn't have missed a second of my moves if I'd been on a ramp at Radlands," he told Jordan.

But Jordan didn't hear. He and Tom were chattering about the possibility of getting a sponsor. Bobby looked over at Petey and said, "Chill, dude. We've got plenty of your radical tricks on tape, and you know we're going to get plenty more."

"I guess," Petey said, unable to meet Bobby's eyes. He was staring at the Pipe Riders, who had cleared a space and were practicing some heavy moves. On Scott's face was his usual smirk—he had already forgotten how Petey had totally creamed him!

Tom and Jordan were still talking excitedly, but Bobby could tell there was something wrong with Petey, who was standing apart from them and still looking away. Bobby walked over to him and said, "You all right?"

Petey turned to him. "Sure, I'm all right. Why shouldn't I be all right?"

"Don't be too hard on Jordan. He was just trying to do us all a favor."

"I know. It's just that—"

"What?"

"Oh, nothing."

"What is it?"

Petey looked away again. "It just seems like you guys look down on me 'cause I'm not into the ramps. I mean, maybe it wasn't any accident that Jordan missed my stunt."

"You know it was an accident." Bobby looked over at Tom and Jordan, who didn't even seem to notice that he and Petey weren't standing with them. "He's just human, like the rest of us."

"Well, that's what I'm tryin' to say. He's just like the rest of you guys. But I'm not. Or at least I don't feel like it."

Bobby looked hard into Petey's eyes and suddenly realized it wasn't just his moves he and the others should have been paying more attention to. "Come on," he said. "Let me get you another Coke or something."

But Petey didn't seem to be listening. Without even looking at Bobby, he picked up his board and walked away.

6

"Got it!" Jordan exclaimed. "This tape is flat out on the cutting edge, and the special effects I dubbed in are awesome." He bent over the lever of his video-editing machine to work on another scene.

"I don't know about the A-bomb explosion and mushroom cloud bit," Bobby said. "Isn't that kind of ... I don't know ... heavy for a skating video?"

"It's rad!" Petey piped in. "People expect to see strange stuff in boarding videos. The atomic blast is heavy—just like rad skating."

"I liked it when you cut from the panther jumping off the tree branch to Bobby shooting down the valley in Ramp 2," Tom said. "When do we get to see the finished version?"

Jordan flicked a switch on the editing board; a whiny hum indicated the machine was working. "In about five minutes," he said. "Soon as the whole thing runs through the board. I've cut the stuff that won't impress a sponsor and kept in all the footage that shows how acute the Wizards skate. I hope you dudes like it."

Minutes later the boys fidgeted nervously in the Kowski living room as Jordan dropped the demo tape into the VCR. "Ready?"

"Come on," Petey groaned. "Don't keep us in suspense any longer."

The television screen flickered to life. First there appeared a shot of a small, tropical island surrounded by calm, clear blue water. Then, the scene seemed to shake. Trees, dirt, rocks, and grass were sucked into a towering, churning column of thick white smoke that rapidly fed into a mushroom cloud. Superimposed across the cloud were the words THE STREET WIZARDS and, under them, SAN CARLOS, CALIFORNIA.

That shot faded slowly, smoke lingering on the screen. Suddenly Bobby was in sharp focus, shooting up the ramp, grabbing air, and spiking an awesome handplant. The scene changed, and Tom appeared on the screen, laying down the same move. Then both boys were on the screen, doing their crossover vert. The Wizards cheered.

A dinosaur appeared in the background, watching Bobby dice at top speed on the ramp, sliding past other skaters as easily as if he were completely alone.

"You're up next, Petey!" Jordan cued. "Watch this!"

Petey skated across the valley from the left of the screen to the right, hung a cool olly, and landed smoothly. The scene cut back to the atomic blast, and the opening words appeared again, as light faded to dark and the video ended.

After the demo ended, a long silence hung over the room.

Finally, Petey stood up from the couch. "Are you serious?" he asked. "That's it for the Wizards' demo?"

"Well . . . yeah," Jordan answered, a little confused. "What's the matter? Didn't you like it?"

"You could have called it the Tom and Bobby Show," Petey snapped. "That would have made more sense. Or maybe Ramp Action 'cause that's all it showed."

"I liked it," Bobby said quietly. "I think it shows what we can do. I think a sponsor will dig it, too."

"Sure," Tom said, stepping over to Petey. "Lighten up, dude. All we want the demo to do is snag us a sponsor. The moves Jordan picked up on will probably do it."

"What about my grind at the Senior Center? You guys didn't think that showed any skill?" Petey asked, his voice flat and hard.

"Of course it did," Bobby answered. "It was really acute. But we don't want to be showing anything that might look too dangerous. The whole point of this tape is to . . ."

". . . get us a sponsor," Petey finished for Bobby, coldly. "We better be real careful that we don't have any fun skating or a sponsor won't like it," he added sarcastically.

Bobby, Tom, and Jordan were quiet for a moment, not sure what to say.

"Look," Bobby finally said. "Let's take the tape to the computer store and let Mr. Trumble have a look at it. Maybe we can get an unbiased opinion from him."

"Good idea," Jordan said, looking at Petey. "And remember, Mr. Trumble told me he used to skate, and he dug empty pools. If he thinks the tape should include some freestyling, he'll say so. Fair enough?"

Petey thought it over for a moment. "Sure," he said without enthusiasm. "Let's go talk to this middle-aged thrasher!"

The Street Wizards skated to Mr. Trumble's store in record time.

"I like it," Trumble told them after watching it. "It's well done and the skateboarding is really exciting. I could picture my store's logo on your T-shirts all during the tape. The thing is, before I commit to paying for your travel and food and so forth, I've got to make sure you fellows are the best skateboarders to represent me."

Trumble hesitated for a moment.

"Tom and Bobby are obviously your ramp experts," he continued. "Mr. Lyons from Radlands told me there's a big competition coming up at his place in a week or so. Here's my offer. If Tom and Bobby both place in the competition, then the Street Wizards have a sponsor. Does that sound fair to you boys?"

"Do you think the demo is missing anything?" Petey asked. "Is there anything you want changed —or added?"

Mr. Trumble thought for a moment. "Nope. It looks just fine to me. Nice job, boys!"

Petey was much quieter than usual after the Wizards left the store. After Bobby put a long, precisely balanced grind on the curb in front of Ralph's Auto Parts on the Main, Petey hit the curb as if he were angry at it, double-trucking, power-grinding way past the spot where Bobby had croaked his own run.

"That made me feel better," Petey admitted. "And I'm glad we're going to run our obstacle course instead of ramping."

Even Jordan took a shot at the curb, and got a little distance. His minicam was safe at home, and he was enjoying the freedom to skate that he'd missed while making the video.

The Street Wizards snaked out to the expressway, crossed over, and set up their obstacle course in the K-mart parking lot. By the time the run was ready, the sun was pounding down mercilessly. They bought drinks from the machine in front of the store, then sat on their boards by the curb, in the shadow of the overhang.

"I saw in the new issue of *Thrasher* that four new skate parks are opening up in California, three in New York, and some more in other states," Bobby said. "Maybe we'll be hitting them all—on the computer store's money."

"It's going to be great passing out Cokes and stuff to other skaters," Tom mused. "Being a pro is going to be double awesome."

"Yeah," Bobby agreed. "Just as long as we don't come on like Corey 'Big Time' Burnhart. That dork's in love with himself."

"He's probably not really such a bad dude," Petey said. "He acts a little stuck on himself at times, but he sure can skate—there's no doubt about that at all."

"Maybe," Bobby allowed, "but the Lion's ramp work is . . ."

Petey was suddenly on his board and shoving off. "Ramp skating! That's all I hear at Radlands, and all I hear from the Street Wizards lately."

He wheeled away from the others into the bright sunlight, rolling in a wide, fast circle around the obstacle course, taking out his anger on the pavement. He poured on speed and then dragged his board to a grinding stop that led to a 360. He pushed out of the 360 and attacked the course.

The first turn was a right angle to the left, and Petey swept it at top speed, setting up for an immediate olly over the tree limb suspended between cinder blocks. He launched his board with a kick downward on its tail and rocketed over the limb with a foot and a half of air to spare. He croaked the olly deliberately, and slammed down onto the hot pavement. Then he forced the board sideways so that it slid into and around the next right angle without losing any power.

"Try that on some lame ramp," he grumbled to himself.

Petey hurtled his board around the final turn of the course, ollied over the half-crushed barrel, and let his board roll to a stop on its own. He felt better after the run, and he wheeled back to try to shave a couple seconds off his time. Halfway through his second shot at the course he veered off into the parking lot for no particular reason except to enjoy the sensation of speed and the cooling breeze against his sweaty face.

He scribed long, snaking lines, shifting his body slightly to control the course of his board.

"We were watching you scorch this run," Bobby said as Petey headed back to the obstacle course. "You looked real tough."

"That olly-to-frontside was awesome," Tom added. "How did you know you'd make it without plowing off-course?"

"It ain't hard if you watch what you're doing," Petey explained. "When you've got your nose up it's easy to swing your weight a little at the same time you shove down. Then, when you hit, you're still rolling good. See what I mean?"

Bobby and Tom looked at one another, shaking their heads.

"No," Tom said.

"Me neither," Bobby said. "Show us."

Petey wheeled out in a long oval to build speed and rushed the course like a runaway express train. "Watch!" he shouted as he launched into an olly. He exaggerated the body motion needed to swing his board onto the right line and powered through the turn smoothly.

Tom tried the run next. He set himself up for the olly but didn't get enough height. When he tried to swing his board he put too much weight into it and lost his balance. He scrambled to catch himself but crashed and burned with an impact that sent him skidding on his kneepads into the rusted end of the barrel. It slammed into his chest, and his breath exploded out of him. He fell on his side red-faced, gasping for air. Petey, Jordan, and Bobby rushed over.

"You OK?" Petey asked, noticing fresh road rash on Tom's right elbow.

"I . . . think so," Tom gasped. He sucked air and tugged the bottom of his Cheap Harold's shirt up to his neck. An angry-looking red welt ran across the upper part of his chest.

"Take a deep breath and see if it hurts," Bobby said.

Tom drew in a long breath and winced.

Bobby looked worried. "I hope you didn't bust a rib or something."

"I didn't," Tom said. "I cracked one playing softball once, and it hurt a lot more than this."

"You've had your tetanus shot, right?" Jordan asked.

Tom nodded, then smiled. "Maybe I should stick to the ramps and leave the hotshot stuff alone."

"Nobody ever gets hurt on a ramp," Petey said cynically.

Tom stood up shakily and lowered his shirt. "Hey, chill out. All I meant was that there aren't a whole lot of rusty bent-up old barrels on the ramps I skate. Sometimes freestyling gets a little out of control. That's all."

Bobby wheeled over to Tom's board, picked it up, and skated back. "Ready for another whack at the course?" he asked.

Tom took his board. "In a few minutes. You

dudes go ahead. I need to catch my breath." He dropped his board and skated off slowly. Jordan rolled after him.

Petey and Bobby stood together awkwardly for a few moments, until Bobby shoved off. He put a solid run on the obstacle course, but Petey noticed he didn't even attempt the midair change of direction that had brought Tom down in smoke and flames.

After a while, Tom skated over and tried the course again. He looked good and ran it fast and hard, but he also avoided the move that had dumped him earlier.

Bobby checked the unbreakable watch he'd gotten for his last birthday. "Getting late. I bet the crowd at Radlands has probably thinned out by now. You dudes want to do some ramping?"

Tom brightened up immediately. "Sure. We need to work some more on our crossover vert."

"Sounds good to me," Jordan said. "What do you think, Petey?"

What Petey thought was that there was a lot more to skating than ramps and ramp moves involving only two guys from a gang. Instead of saying what he thought, though, he forced a lame smile.

"Does that mean yes?" Bobby asked. He had tried to conceal the sarcasm in his voice, but he didn't succeed. Petey had been making him so angry lately that he couldn't control it any longer.

"Whatever you say, boss," Petey replied.

"Listen, dude," Bobby said, skating up alongside him and talking too quietly for Jordan and Tom to hear. "You need a major attitude adjustment here."

"Oh, yeah? And I guess you're the one to help me out with it, right?"

"Maybe I am," Bobby said, more loudly than he had intended. Jordan and Tom were looking in their direction.

"Then I'll take a rain check," Petey said, and, pumping hard with his foot against the pavement, skated away.

7

Petey rode down the Main keeping tight to the curb, laying down an occasional grind or ollying over gum wrappers or other garbage dropped by careless pedestrians. He had no exact destination in mind, but he knew the general direction he wanted to take—away from Radlands.

He tromped the tail of his board to rocket over a crack in the sidewalk, touched down, and pumped to keep up his momentum. The blare of a horn startled him and he skidded to a stop.

Next to the curb the black Cable 7 van sat idling. Mike McGee leaned out of the passenger's side window, smiling with all of his six thousand gleaming white teeth.

"Hey, Slick, how come you're not dicing with your pals at Radlands?"

Petey swallowed the smart remark that immediately popped into his head, wondering what the dude wanted with him after their scene the other day.

"I felt like crankin' some freestyling," he answered. "Radlands gets a little crowded with all the pros and out-of-town skaters."

"Not your scene? Don't tell me you're a thrasher who's out to terrorize the streets."

Petey put a foot down to shove off.

"Hey, dude, I was only kidding you," Mike McGee called out quickly. "Look, I was hot the other day, but I've got to admit you nailed me right to the wall. Not many people can nail the baddest emcee, I'll lay that on you. But if your freestyle skating's half as cool as people say, it's got to be something to see. And I dig that you don't stick in the park all day, rolling the same scores."

Petey was a bit confused by all this. "So?"

"Point is, I'm shooting some film about real skating. You know, like what goes down on the streets, not at Radlands."

"Why tell me about it?"

"My, my," Mike McGee said, laughing. "Hostile today, aren't we? That's OK. It's part of your style. I just thought I'd stop and tell you that a whole herd of skaters who do things your way are rolling over at MacArthur Park, by that dynamite old fountain."

He saw that he'd gotten Petey's attention. "You get into fountains? So do the other board crazies there."

"Like who?"

"Burn's there, and that knockout chick Heidi and those guys who call themselves the Pipe Riders. You know them, don't you?"

"Yeah, sure I know them," Petey said. "Who else?"

"Kind of interested, huh, Slick?" Mike asked.

"Maybe," Petey admitted. "Who else is there?"

"A bunch of those kids who look like they were just coughed up by a cat. I guess most of them are out-of-towners here for Megarad." The emcee swung open the door of the van. "Pile in, Slick. We'll ride you to the park."

"I'll skate. Thanks anyway."

"Have it your way, dude. Catch you later." The van burned rubber away from the curb and blasted off down the Main.

Petey couldn't help smiling. Mike McGee had probably just beaten him for an interview that he'd edit any way he wanted, and the baddest emcee would come out looking like King of the Boarders.

But when he began skating again he picked up his pace and didn't waste time thinking about anything that might slow him down.

Petey heard the music long before he reached the fountain. Several boom boxes were blaring, each playing a different tape or hooked into a different station. The sidewalks that led through the park were wide and level, but unfortunately, didn't have curbs. Still, the gentle curves allowed a skater to crank on speed and hold it as he or she snaked along. Petey fired out of a long turn and let his board roll to a stop as he scoped what was happening.

The fountain looked like a gigantic cement Frisbee that had been tossed upside down onto an acre of pavement. It was about a hundred feet across and not much deeper than a couple of feet at its lowest point, in the very center. The floor of the dry fountain curved up gradually to the edge, which was the kind of curb skaters would die for. Kids were cutting back and forth in the basin, grinding along the long, curving rim, spiking ollies in the basin—doing whatever came to mind and having a ball. Corey Burnhart, surrounded by skaters—mostly girls—was demonstrating freestyle moves on the plaza around the fountain. Mike McGee walked around with a microphone in his hand. A guy with a video camera was right behind him taping.

Mike McGee waved to Petey. "Glad to see you, Slick. Gonna give my man here something to tape? I'll connect with you in a few—Burn is doing some stuff I need for my show."

Mike McGee and his cameraman hustled off to where Corey Burnhart was boarding. Petey rolled in the same direction until a voice stopped him.

"Hey, Marino! What's the matter. Radlands burn down or something?" Scott Longo brayed with laughter at his own joke. Brad Munson, at his side, laughed just as hard. Scott dragged to a sliding stop next to Petey's board. "The rest of the Wizards here?"

"Just me," Petey answered. He began to skate away.

"Hey," Scott said, "I heard you dorks were making a video. Give up on it yet?" He laughed again. "Watching the Street Wizards skate ramps is about as interesting as watching a tree grow."

"Maybe you guys can rent it from us," Petey said. "If you watch it enough times, you might even learn to skate."

"Yeah, right," Scott said. "I'd learn how to skate up and down a ramp. Big deal. Me and the Pipe Riders dig more action than we can get on the ramps?"

"What kind of action?"

"Street action, dude! Freestyling. The kind of stuff fresh cuts get warned about by their mothers. Of course, the Wizards don't know anything about that."

Brad had to get in his two cents' worth. "I didn't think old man Lyons and his kid Superwimp let you Wizards take your boards out of Radlands," he sneered.

Petey was about to fire off an answer when loud cheering and applause caught his attention.

Scott turned to the sound as well. "Hey! Burn is struttin' his stuff in the fountain!"

Corey Burnhart seemed to roll full out at top speed, no matter what he was doing. He laid a grind on the fountain edge that sent up a cloud of cement dust. He nosed into the fountain after croaking the grind, ollied, then spun himself and his board in a 360 in midair. He came down like an arrow striking a target, scraping along for several feet on the nose of his board. Then, using what was left of his momentum, he flicked his weight quickly to his left, straightened, and was rolling smoothly in a fakie.

"Awesome!" Petey shouted.

Everyone else had the same reaction. Burnhart smiled at the applause and the cheers. "You come to skate or to gawk?" he demanded. "There's lots of room in here for anybody who wants to get it on!"

Petey was one of the first to hit the fountain. He caught Burnhart's eye when he careened down the sidewalk, ollied over the edge, and came down in the basin.

"Not bad!" the older skater said. "You got any more moves, kid?"

"I think I might have one or two more." Petey grinned, shoving off across the basin, snaking so hard that the tail of his board skidded when he cut back and forth. He whipped into a backside turn past the metal sprayer, wheeled around hard, and pumped as he raced toward it.

The sprayer was shaped roughly like a fire hydrant, but came to a sharp peak and was drilled with hundreds of holes. Petey leaned back, tromped the tail of his board, and launched himself at the small metal stump. He spiked the move, the center of his board slamming onto the sprayer's peak. He spread his feet on his deck, separating them as far as he could, and at the same time whipping his body in the direction of his thrust.

For a long moment, he spun on the peak like a propeller. He hauled his tail foot forward on the deck. Then he and his board plunged off the sprayer and back into the basin.

"Man," Corey roared, "a gen-u-ine freestyler right here in Wimpton, California!"

"Roll some more, Slick!" Mike McGee hollered. "I got you covered!" The cameraman, standing shakily on the lip of the fountain, had taped every inch of Petey's run.

Petey, gasping for air, coasted to where Burnhart stood. "What do you think?" Petey asked.

The pro slapped him on the shoulder. "I could purely dig it, man. Come on, I want to show you something."

A crowd of skaters surged out into the basin with them. Heidi shot up next to them, and so did some of the other pros who had been skating in San Carlos lately.

"Dig this!" Corey yelled, sailing off toward the sprayer. He cut around it at the last possible fraction of a second, grabbed the peak with one hand and the lip of his board with the other, made a complete revolution, and let go. He rocketed through the air, scrambling to right his board—and did it. He hit hard and swung into a broadside duster, skidding backside first. Skaters who were charging into the fountain from the other side leaped, skated, or dove out of his path. Mike McGee and his cameraman were ecstatic.

Petey wiped sweat from his forehead and powered farther out into the basin, cutting in front of several other skaters. He raced to the quadrant of the fountain that was least crowded, pumping to build speed. He rocketed up the gentle slope, gauged the distance, and shifted his weight to one side so that the edge of his board closest to the lip rose into the air.

Then, Petey shifted his weight again, dropping the board so that two wheels—one front and one rear—were on the lip. He tweaked the ride a shade too long and had to bail out to avoid going down in flames. His board skittered away, and Petey stood there gulping air, riding his adrenaline rush.

Burnhart and Bobby Clark reached Petey at the

same time. "Outtasight!" the pro said. "Boss grind, man." Then he skated off, in Heidi's direction.

Petey was surprised to see Bobby. "Where'd you . . ."

"We came looking for you," Bobby said. "Then we heard about the deal here, and we figured this is where you'd be."

"Awesome, isn't it?"

At that moment a scream split the air. A girl had been hit in the leg by a flying board. A skater had been trying to copy Petey's right-angle grind and lost it.

"I . . . I don't know," Bobby said. "Looks like things are getting pretty hairy here."

Jordan and Tom skated up with Petey's board. "You ready to split, Petey?" Jordan asked.

"No, I'm not ready to split!" Petey snapped. "All these dudes think my freestyling is dynamite and you guys want to leave. Are you jealous or something? I don't try to drag you away when you're riding that stupid ramp, do I?"

"Hey, come on," Bobby said. "I'm sorry about the way I acted back there in the parking lot. I . . . I was just feeling a little crazy."

Petey looked at him but didn't reply.

"We know your street skating's awesome," Bobby went on. "But this is crazy! Someone's gonna get wrecked stunting in the fountain."

As if to back up Bobby's words, two fast-moving

freestylers came together with a terrific crash that left them both moaning on the basin floor.

Jordan stepped between Petey and Bobby. "I know you've felt kind of . . . I don't know . . . left out lately, Petey. But Bobby's probably right. These kids are gonna kill each other. Some of these pros are whacked out. They don't care what happens to them or to anyone else. That Digger Sneaks dude just took out a couple of fresh cuts who weren't fast enough to get out of his way."

"Maybe the fresh cuts should have been skating at Radlands, then," Petey said. "I don't want to see anybody get hurt any more than you guys do, but this is the type of skating I really dig."

He looked around the fountain, his eyes gleaming. "Look at all this—music, lots of skaters, heavy moves, tricks I never seen before—this is the way skateboarding's supposed to be. It's a lot more fun!"

"But Petey . . ." Jordan began.

He was cut short by the shrill rasping of whistles. Four policemen raced toward the fountain on foot from four different directions.

"All you punks stop right where you are!" one of them roared.

The skateboarders jumped on their boards and took off like a flock of birds at the blast of a shotgun, wheeling down the sidewalks, ollying over benches—anything to escape. The Wizards separated in the mad rush. Petey skated down one of the sidewalks that radiated out diagonally from the fountain, but the whistling grew louder. It was coming from one whistle in particular—the one in the mouth of the cop who was hard on his heels!

"Hey, Marino, this way!" a voice said.

Petey turned and saw Scott, who had caught up with him and was motioning for him to skate onto an asphalt-paved path intersecting the sidewalk. Petey was suspicious; he thought it might be a trick. But the street was still far away, and he didn't seem to have any choice, so he followed Scott down the path, which curved between huge gnarled oaks and led to a patch of azaleas. Scott hopped off his board, picked it up, then dove for cover in the bushes. Petey followed. They lay there panting, listening to the whistling grow more and more distant.

"Didn't take much to lose those squid guards, did it?" Scott asked when he had caught his breath.

"Where's Munson and your other guys?"

Scott looked around. "Beats me. Maybe they're with your guys. Hey, outtasight freestylin' in there, dude. You got some heavy moves—too heavy for those dudes you run with." He grinned at Petey. "Wanna get a Coke and a hot dog or something and then do some street riding?"

A Street Wizard riding with a Pipe Rider? Petey

thought it over for a moment. It sounded pretty outrageous, but at least he wasn't being ragged on for his freestyle skating.

"Why not?" Petey said, climbing onto his skateboard and pushing off.

8

"Shoot!" Brad howled as his board shot out from under him and he hit the pavement hard. They were skating the curb in front of the Discount Furniture Mart on the Main. Petey had put a long, fast power grind on it. Scott, a board's length behind him, had croaked his grind before hanging the distance Petey had achieved. Brad just sat there dazed, rubbing fresh patches of road rash on his forearms and thighs. "You OK?" Petey asked, coming up to him.

"Why wouldn't I be?" Brad asked.

Petey extended a hand to help him up, but Brad just looked at it and scowled. Then, grim-faced and embarrassed, he picked himself up from the pavement and walked to his board, which had landed upside down against the curb.

"This thing ain't worth the wood it's made out of," Brad grumbled. He kicked his board and immediately wished he hadn't. The toe of his sneaker offered no protection against the hard laminated lip of the skateboard. He howled with pain and grabbed his foot.

"There isn't anything wrong with that board," Scott chided. "It's just that you can't skate worth a piece of chewed gum, Bradley."

Brad turned on Petey, since he didn't dare flap his mouth too much at Scott. "What're you smilin' about, dork?" he demanded. "At least I got a gang to skate with."

"What's that supposed to mean, Munson?" Petey growled. "I got a gang."

"Sure you do—when you're at Radlands doing ups and downs on the ramp. When you want to freestyle, you run with the Pipe Riders—like you been doin' for the past couple of days."

"You got a problem with me skatin' with the Pipe Riders? Last time I heard, Scott was the leader of this gang."

Eddie Tedesco, who was a decent skater, stopped his board and said to Petey, "Don't listen to him. We're glad to have you doing stuff with us. Your moves are heavy—and that reverse you showed me yesterday is real easy since you explained it."

Brad wasn't ready to drop the matter. "I guess them dweeb Street Wizards booted you outta their gang. That's why you're skatin' with . . ."

Petey cut hard and skidded to a stop in front of Brad. "Listen, dork," he growled, "I'm still a Street Wizard. I'm just a little sick of ramps and pipes— but that isn't any of your business. I'm getting real tired of your mouth. For a squid who skates like he started yesterday you make too much noise."

Brad wasn't going to back down in front of the other Pipe Riders.

"Sounds to me like you don't have a gang, Marino. The Wizards don't want you, and you don't skate good enough for the Pipe Riders. Maybe you should . . ."

Petey was off his board in a flash. He grabbed the front of Brad's T-shirt with one hand, ready to whack him with the other.

Scott pushed the two boys apart. "Knock it off, Munson, or you're gonna get your face scrambled. Lay off of Petey, dig? The dude can skate—which is a lot more than I can say about you. And he's got some guts, too."

"I've got guts!" Brad insisted. "I can do anything that Marino can do . . ."

"Aw, pack it," Scott snorted. "Come on, Petey, let's lay a grind on the railing over by the library." The skaters set off again, their ragged snake line taking over a lot more of the sidewalk than Petey was used to skating on. When Scott ollied over a Scottish terrier on a leash held by an elderly woman, she snapped, "You young thug! Mayor Lowery is going to hear about this! Those skateboards ought to be outlawed in this town!"

"So should crummy little pooches like that rat-on-a-string you're draggin' around!" Scott retorted. The woman glared at Scott, and Petey was sure she wouldn't forget exactly what he looked like for a long time—like not until after the next Parents Against Skateboarding meeting.

As the boys swung down a side street, Heidi and several pro groupies shot around a corner toward them.

"Petey! Scott!" Heidi called. "Boy, I'm glad we ran into you dudes! We've found the hairiest place in the whole world to skate!"

"Where?" Scott asked, immediately interested.

"Out by that unfinished stretch of highway outside of town. There's . . ."

". . . not much out there but flat cement and sand and . . ." Petey said.

"Wrong! If you go way out, there's a bridge between a couple of hills with a road under it and a really heavy slope that—" Heidi stopped and stepped off her board. She picked up a pebble from the street and began to scratch on the sidewalk with it.

"See, here are the hills, and here's the bridge between them. The freeway goes right under the

89

bridge, about sixty feet or so below it. Hanging under the bridge is a little walkway about as wide as a sidewalk. They must use it to work on the bottom of the bridge. It's actually two walkways, one shooting down from either end of the bridge. See, there's this open space right in the middle. Dig it?"

"How do you ride it?" Scott asked.

"Lower down onto the walkway from the bridge, roll hard going down the curve—then hang a frontside air over the open space onto the walkway on the other side! It's the most acute run in the world!"

"Awesome!" Petey said. "But what happens if you blow the frontside air?"

"You make a little wet spot on the freeway." Heidi grinned. "That's part of what makes this place such a mega-rush! I had to leave to call my sponsor to tell him I wouldn't be at Radlands until later— we're heading back to the bridge now."

Petey and Scott's eyes met. "Can you dig it?" Petey asked.

"You bet I can!" Scott answered. "Let's roll!"

The unfinished highway was generally as quiet as a tomb. Today, however, a big crowd of radical skaters, fresh cuts, and groupies were partying and skating on the hillside around the bridge. Petey could make out the Shooters from their hot-pink clothes. Music blared from several boom boxes, and the buzzing hum of skateboard wheels scorching cement filled the hot, still air.

Petey gulped as he and the Pipe Riders skated up. The bridge hulked between the hills, its weathered cement a flat, dull gray, its metal cables rusted and pitted. Petey felt a quick chill as he scoped out the structure—and the highway below.

Corey Burnhart waved to the admiring crowd of groupies and skaters below him. He lowered himself over the side railing, hung by one hand for the moment it took to slap his board under his feet, and let go. He dropped about four feet to the four-foot-wide walkway and shot down it like a rocket-powered sled. He whooped loudly enough to be heard above the music.

"Mega-rad! Awesome! This is the gnarliest run I've ever done!" Toward the bottom of the arc Burnhart set up for a frontside air, grabbed a ton of air as he shot across five feet of totally open space, and touched down on the walkway on the other side with a lurch. His board skittered for a fraction of a second before he snagged control of it. His back wheels hung off in space for a heartbeat, with nothing between them and the highway below but sixty feet of open air. He gulped as he straightened out, then whooped again.

"That's one run I'm gonna make no matter what!" Petey yelled excitedly.

The groupies cheered Burnhart. Many of the skaters rushed to the bridge to be next to drop down for a run. Heidi pushed to the front of the crowd, and everyone made way for her.

"Think she'll try a frontside air like Burn did?" asked a thrasher standing next to Petey.

"Either that or spend the rest of her life out there," Petey answered. "There ain't no other way off, except to call the Fire Department to bring a ladder."

Chelsea McIntyre, Mandy, and the other Shooters skated to a stop beside Petey and the Pipe Riders. "Pretty hairy," Chelsea said to Petey. "We're taking off. Hey, I think Bobby, Tom, and Jordan are over at Radlands. Want to come with us? It's, like, too dangerous to hang out here."

"Are you kidding?" Scott broke in before Petey could answer. "The dude's waiting his turn up there, aren't you, Petey?"

Petey looked from Scott to Chelsea. "Uhh, sure," he answered hesitantly.

Chelsea looked as if she were about to say something, but stopped herself and shrugged instead. "It's your brain. I'd just hate to see it splattered all over the freeway down there. See ya later."

"Come on, dudes," Scott called out, motioning Petey and the other Pipe Riders closer to the bridge. "Check out what Heidi's doing."

She eased over the side, dropped as gently as a

cat to the surface of the walkway, and shot downward like an arrow from the world's most powerful bow. Her smile faltered for half a second when she saw there was no turning back. But when she lowered her body for even more speed and she plunged downward, her smile returned, broader than ever. Her frontside air was picture perfect. Her landing was even smoother than Burnhart's had been. Cheers rose into the hot summer air again.

Petey caught sight of hot pink T-shirts and shorts on the far side of the crowd. Chelsea and the Shooters were heading back toward town. He watched them for a moment and then turned back to the action.

Another pro dropped onto the walkway from the bridge. She powered down the slope like a bullet, and kicked her board and her body into a fakie that sent her hurtling backward to the jump point. Then she launched off in a backside air, tweaked the move with a quick smile, and waved at the kids staring up at her. She landed dead center on the other side of the walkway. Petey heaved a big sigh of relief.

"That chick has more guts than a slaughterhouse!" Scott exclaimed. "Man, I'd dig having her in the Pipe Riders."

Eddie Tedesco nodded in agreement. "Our rep would be even heavier than it is now!"

"She ain't all that awesome," Brad said with a sneer. "All she did was a twist and a backside air. That ain't no big deal. Any fresh cut could..."

"All she did?" Scott asked with disbelief. "You couldn't cut those moves in a parking lot, much less about a million feet above that road down there."

Brad's face turned scarlet. "I can..."

"Pack it, will you?" Scott said. "Maybe Marino was right—you're all mouth, man. There's nothing behind your talk."

Brad picked up his board, his hands trembling with anger. He began to say something, stopped, then began to walk away, grumbling to himself.

Petey shook his head as he watched Brad walk away. "I know the guy's a dork, but you come down awful hard on him. Especially since he is a Pipe Rider."

"The dude's a zero," Scott said, laughing. "The only reason he's in my gang is because he lives on the same block as me and Eddie. Forget about that dweeb. Let's go up on the bridge and get in line."

Brad stopped walking when he could no longer hear their voices. The bridge loomed ahead of him. On one side, a crowd of skaters argued over who was going to go next. Brad shuddered a bit. Then he squared his shoulders and began up the hill.

"I'll show those dorks," he growled under his

breath. "Nobody's gonna bust my chops after I'm finished runnin' that walkway faster and tighter than Burn or that chick did. I've got solid-steel nerves." He swallowed hard. "And I'm not scared of high places."

He hesitated, then kept moving up the hill to the bridge. His board almost slipped from his hand because of the sweat on his palm. *I'm not scared,* he told himself over and over again. *I'm not scared.*

As Petey, Scott, and Eddie headed toward the bridge, they heard a ruckus from the crowd of skaters gathered on the hillside near the drop-off.

As he peered at the cement walkway under the bridge, Petey's mouth dropped. "Holy cats! That's Brad up there!"

Brad, his face drained white from fear, half-stood and half-crouched where he'd dropped onto the walkway from the bridge. He couldn't climb back up because of the steepness of the angle, and he was too scared even to think of riding the slope on his board. His fear-widened eyes were drawn to the freeway pavement baking in the sun sixty feet below. He watched in horror as a pebble that had lodged in the sole of one of his sneaks dropped free and plunged toward the road below. It struck the concrete in a little puff of dust that sent another chill up his spine.

Cold, clammy sweat dripped into his eyes. He stared downward. He wanted to look away, but couldn't. He felt like a mouse staring into the eyes of a hungry rattlesnake. Suddenly, he felt very, very alone.

9

Back at Radlands, Bobby rolled out of a hand-plant, his wheels clicking down solidly on the slope of Ramp 2. Tom, a half-second behind him, flashed a raised fist.

"Outtasight!" he yelled.

Bobby started to reply when Chelsea McIntyre grabbed onto his arm with a vicelike grip. Her eyes were frantic, and her voice shook as she spoke.

"Bobby," she said, "I'm scared there's going to be big trouble. Petey is out at the overpass on the unfinished highway, and the skaters there are doing really weird stuff on the bridge over the freeway. Petey said he was going to run it. We skated back here to get you guys."

Quickly, Bobby motioned to Jordan and Tom. As they rolled over, Bobby squeezed Chelsea's hand. "Thanks," he said. "You did the right thing." When the other two Street Wizards pulled up, Chelsea filled them in on what was happening.

"Maybe we should go over there and stop him,"

Jordan said, obviously as concerned as Chelsea.

"Stop Petey?" Tom exclaimed. "You've got to be joking. He won't even skate with us anymore."

"So whose fault is that?" Chelsea asked. "You guys always want to ramp-skate, and Petey's one of the best freestylers anywhere."

For a moment the three Wizards were silent. Tom took a deep breath. "Maybe we should check it out and make sure he's OK."

"I'm for that," Bobby seconded. "Come on guys, we don't have any time to waste."

Back at the overpass, Petey hung from the bridge by one hand, gripping his board tightly in the other. "I'm gonna drop right next to you," he called out to Brad as calmly as he could. Like Brad's, his eyes were drawn to the road, far below the bridge. He turned away.

"Don't sweat it. We'll get you out of this," Petey said, with more confidence than he felt. His voice trembled a bit, and he hoped Brad hadn't heard it.

Petey let go and dropped, skidding on the soles of his sneaks, straight down the walkway. Finally, he stopped, about a yard below where Brad was standing.

"You gotta quit looking down. Come on, look at me." Petey forced a laugh. "Not that we get along so great or anything, but wouldn't you rather look at me than that stretch of road down there?"

Brad's eyes remained glued to the freeway. Petey noticed how pale Brad was—his entire body was quivering with fear. Petey had to do something very soon. If he didn't, Brad was going to shake himself right off the walkway.

"You ever wonder how you can tell if a dinosaur's been in your refrigerator?" Petey asked, trying to make his voice sound as light as possible.

Brad's eyes flicked up to Petey's face, as if he couldn't believe he had chosen that moment to tell a joke.

"Great! Now don't look back down!" Petey instructed quickly.

Brad nodded slowly, keeping his eyes fixed on Petey's face.

Petey decided to keep the joke going. "All you gotta do is check the butter for dinosaur tracks."

"I'm gonna fall," Brad croaked.

"You're not gonna fall," Petey said quietly. "Quit thinking like that!"

Brad groaned. "I . . . I'm getting dizzy. I . . ."

Petey stole an upward glance. A line of faces silently started down at him. For once, Corey Burnhart's tan seemed to have faded. Before he had even turned away from the other skaters, Petey could sense Brad's fear. He could *feel* Brad's body trembling, as if he were causing the entire walkway to shake!

Petey swallowed several times so that his voice

wouldn't crack midsentence. He tried to keep his tone light, but it sounded phony, even to him. "Look, Brad, here's what we're going to do. I've had time to figure out this run and you haven't, so I'll talk you through it. OK?"

"I . . . I can't. I'm scared." Brad's voice was so low Petey could barely hear it.

"Pack that stuff about bein' scared!" Petey ordered. "Just listen to me and do what I say. Understand?"

For a fraction of a second Brad looked even more frightened. Petey was afraid he'd blown it, until Brad nodded his head slightly.

"OK," he whispered.

"Good," Petey went on. "The first thing's just a straight run down this slope. It'll be fast, but no big deal. Then, when you get about halfway, you start to set up for a frontside air. That's no big deal, either. You can do it, right?"

Brad nodded slightly.

"Good. The frontsider will put you out grabbin' some air, and that'll take you right over the gap. Then you land on the far walkway, and ride your speed up to where you can grab one of those iron bars on the bottom of the bridge. That's about all there is to it, dude. You ready to give it a try?" Petey swallowed hard, trying to ignore the nervousness building in his stomach.

100

Brad didn't answer. He just stared at Petey, looking white as a ghost.

"Brad? Am I talking to myself out here? Answer me, dude!"

"You ... you go first and let me watch," Brad rasped. "P-p-p-please, Marino. I'll do it after you."

Petey thought for a second and then made his decision. "Sure," he said. "Watch real carefully now." He pasted a big artificial smile on his face. Then he reached up, slugged Brad lightly on the shoulder, and stepped onto his board.

He knew the other boy's life depended on his moves. He crouched low on his board to make balancing less difficult. Petey careened downward and set himself up for the frontside air. In spite of his crouch, the speed was breathtaking. He shot out into space, soaring over the gap. It seemed like forever before his board touched down on the walkway on the other side. Petey grabbed onto an iron girder and held it tightly, locking his feet around his skateboard so it wouldn't roll away. Then he called over to Brad. It was now or never.

"Your turn! There's nothin' to it. Go, dude! Hit it!"

Brad's face was snow-white. On the bridge and below there was no sound but the breeze sighing through the iron cables. None of the spectators said a word, not even when Bobby, Tom, and Jordan pulled up and ran onto the bridge to watch. Brad shifted his feet and stepped onto his board. The skaters were so mesmerized that some of them forgot to breathe.

Brad's board wobbled a bit as he shot down the slope. His mouth was wide open, but no sound came from it. He lurched into the air at the gap instead of soaring over it, as Petey had done. He seemed to lumber through space, barely clearing the gap. His board banged down hard, but somehow he stayed on it, slamming into Petey, who was still hanging tightly from the girder.

Petey snagged the other boy in a clumsy hug. Brad's board shot out into the air. It toppled end over end in a long, slow fall, and splintered into hundreds of pieces the moment it hit the concrete sixty feet below.

"You did it!" Petey roared over the deafening cheers from the other skaters overhead. "You did it!"

When Petey and Brad climbed onto the bridge, Bobby, Tom, and Jordan were the first to mob them. They beat Petey on the back, whooping and yelling.

"You're a hero, dude!" Heidi shrieked, racing forward and planting a big kiss on Petey's cheek. The crowd surged around him, cheering and hugging him, everyone talking and yelling at the same time.

Petey pulled Bobby's head close to his face and shouted over the racket, "After that, ramping's going to look awfully good!"

"Maybe," Bobby hollered into Petey's ear. "But freestyling's a lot harder—and hairier!"

"You got that one hundred percent right, dude! The action here was way too hairy—even for me!"

10

Corey Burnhart was set and ready to roll from the platform on Ramp 4. He glared over at Mike McGee, who was announcing, hoping he'd finish up with his hype sometime before Christmas. He wanted to strut his moves while he still felt the racer's edge—the feeling that the run coming up was going to be flat-out perfect.

"Here's a dude I know personally, friends," Mike McGee's voice crackled through the loudspeakers. "And believe me, I know all of these fine young men and women personally. Make sure you check out my show on Cable 7—you'll see skating the way it *really* is. And I'll introduce you to the hottest, most radical skateboarders in the sport. That's *The World of Skateboarding,* on Cable 7—dig it!

"Now Corey Burnhart's friends—like me—call him Burn. I suppose that's because this honcho purely burns holes in a ramp with the hottest moves it's ever been my good fortune to see! Let's hear it for Corey Burnhart!"

The Street Wizards, swept away by the excitement of the competition, applauded more loudly than anyone else. They were in the front line of the crowd who had gathered at Radlands for Megarad. Each of the boys had a competitor's number pinned to the back of his T-shirt, and they stared with fascination into Ramp 4 as they clapped. They were waiting for the action to begin—for Burnhart to show the stuff he was famous for.

Burnhart shot down the slope as the applause washed over him. His skating clothes were bright white, and his tan, his sandy blond hair, and his sparkling teeth made him look like a California travel poster.

"Here he goes with a tight little olly," McGee said. "Look at that dude move! Here's a vert with lots of power—he's grabbing a ton of air ... and a smooth fakie ... he's rolling hard and laying down an outtasight grind with heavy distance. Isn't his style awesome? The dude's a machine— look at that! A super McTwister! He's got more speed than a highway-patrol pursuit car! Dig it! Now he's setting up for one of his really big moves ... he's wheeling hard, scorching that ramp ... here he goes ... look at that vert! He absolutely touched the sky. And look at that—that's the way a handplant wants to be done, ladies and gents!

"He's tweaking that plant for all it's worth ...

105

here he goes again, tough speed on the slope, dynamite position on his board ... a little frontside turn and then a backsider down there in the valley. Up he goes again—just like a Patriot missile—getting a whole lot of air ... and now a fakie and a short olly that set him up for a sliding stop. And that's it for my buddy Corey Burnhart—the dude called Burn throughout the wonderful world of skateboarding, which I cover every week on Cable 7—don't miss *The World of Skateboarding*!"

The applause all but drowned out Mike McGee's plug for his show. Burnhart, his shirt plastered to his back and chest, waved to the crowd. Several girls sighed loudly enough to be heard through Mike's microphone, and the crowd got a laugh out of it.

"That guy is as smooth as grease," Tom said to the other Street Wizards.

"I didn't see a single move that wasn't perfect," Bobby seconded. "McGee is right—he is a machine."

"Dig it," Petey said in a voice that was very close to Mike McGee's. "You can see my good, good friend Burn on my show on Cable 7! And whatever you do, ladies and gents—don't forget for a second that I'm Mike McGee, the world's baaaadest emcee."

The Wizards cracked up, and so did the rest of

the crowd near enough to Petey to hear the impersonation.

Bobby's laughter stopped in a hurry.

"There's been a little change in the old sequence here," McGee announced over the microphone. "Short Dan from Fresno, skating for the Lame Duck Board Shop—a real close friend of mine—isn't gonna make it today. So we're going to a hot young dude from right here in San Carlos—Bobby Clark! Bobby heads up a gang called the Street Wizards. Bobby's a real tight friend of mine, and I've seen him grow up on that skateboard of his. Let's hear it for Bobby Clark—top gun of the Street Wizards, right here in San Carlos!"

Bobby dropped into the half-pipe and took the cut down the slope hard and fast. He pumped as he started up the opposite slope, and angled his board a few inches as he shot up toward the coping. He tapped the rear of his board and lifted the trucks onto the rim, laying down a long grind. He tweaked the move nicely, croaking it before his speed gave out.

The excellent grind cleared everything but the ramp from Bobby's mind. The familiar rush of shooting down the slope of the ramp, as if he were dropping in a fast elevator, struck him, and he grinned. The breeze felt cool on his face.

Bobby pumped in the valley and rocketed up

the slope. He dropped into a half-crouch and grabbed the lip of his board firmly, his fingers falling into position on the lengths of fresh friction tape he'd applied the night before. In a split second, he hurtled past the coping and continued on into the California sky, grabbing lots of air. His right hand shot down and locked onto the coping. His momentum carried his body until it stood at the end of his arm, his board pressed tightly against the soles of his skating sneakers.

He tweaked every possible second out of the handplant, sticking his chest out a bit more and holding the plant until the last possible millisecond. He came down smoothly, his skateboard wheels hissing against the ramp. Then he cut sharply, and spiked an olly that was awesome in length, height, and style. Applause erupted from the audience. He skidded his board sideways after touching down and stood next to it, waving at the cheering spectators. He stood in the valley looking up expectantly at the emcee.

"A dude named Tom Garcia—another Street Wizard, and another good friend of mine—is going to join Bobby down there for a little trick they call a crossover vert," Mike McGee announced. "Let's welcome Tom Garcia!"

Tom dropped into the half-pipe and fired down the slope, past Bobby, and up the other side. Bobby shoved off and began building speed, cutting up and down the ramp, higher with each run. Tom laid down a handplant that was a little shaky, but didn't look half bad. Bobby worked up speed as Tom ran through an olly and a couple of reverses and fakies. Then the boys nodded to one another and began their runs.

They careened up the slope about eight feet apart, their boards angled slightly toward each other. They left the coping behind them at precisely the same moment and shot past each other with perfect timing. Petey and Jordan began the whooping and cheering, but they weren't alone for long. The crossover vert had been radical, and the audience appreciated the skill it showed.

Burnhart clapped Bobby on the shoulder as he and Tom left the half-pipe. "Awesome skating," he said. "Your routine was outtasight, and the crossover went down real well."

Bobby nodded his thanks and joined the other Street Wizards to wait for the start of the next skater's routine. He turned when he felt a hand on his shoulder, and found a middle-aged dude in a business suit standing behind him. The man nodded toward a quiet place away from the ramp, and handed Bobby a business card. It read, LANCE J. TREVOR, DIGGER RUNNING SHOE COMPANY. In smaller print it read, PROMOTIONAL ADVERTISING REPRESENTATIVE.

When they were away from the crowd, Mr.

Trevor didn't waste time or words. "I like your style. I might have a spot for you in my stable."

"Stable?" Bobby asked.

"What I meant," Mr. Trevor said, smiling, "is that I'm considering recommending that Digger sponsor you, like we do Corey Burnhart and several other people. Are you interested, Bobby? It would mean lots of interesting travel, skating at places you've only read about, things like that."

"I . . . don't know, Mr. Trevor. This is kind of sudden."

"Sure it is. Give it some thought, but not too much—the world's full of hot new talent. I'll be in touch." Mr. Trevor walked back to the ramp, leaving Bobby standing there holding the business card.

As he walked back to rejoin his gang, Bobby passed Mr. Trevor and Corey Burnhart, their heads together, both of them talking fast.

"I don't want to add another olly, Mr. Trevor. My routine doesn't need it. It wouldn't fit—it'd just slow me down and . . ."

Mr. Trevor's voice was quiet but firm. "I said I wanted a final olly in there—and that's what I want to see when you go on again. You hear me? Just remember, Digger picked you up and Digger can drop you just as easily."

Bobby paused for a moment and felt a strange chill crawl up his spine. Maybe having a heavy-duty sponsor wasn't everything it was made out to be.

He told Tom, Petey, and Jordan what Mr. Trevor had said to him. Before they even had a chance to be amazed, he told them what he'd overheard him say to Corey Burnhart. The Wizards looked concerned.

"It's Burnhart's trick, it should be Burnhart's decision what goes in and what doesn't," Petey said.

"Maybe with these big-time sponsors, what should be and what really is are two different things," Jordan said.

"Doesn't sound like much fun to me," Petey added. "Having some dude in a suit tell me how to skate isn't my idea of a good time."

Bobby nodded in agreement.

The crowd on the ramp platform was breaking up and moving to the venue for the freestyle events. Mike McGee was interviewing Heidi, telling the crowd that she was a close personal friend of his. The Street Wizards grinned as they saw the confused look on her face. She'd probably talked to the dude once in her life, and then only for a sixty-second interview.

Petey swallowed hard when he heard his name called over the loudspeaker. Skating freestyle was one thing. Doing it in front of a trillion other people, most of whom were skaters themselves, was something else.

111

He skated in wide, looping circles on the huge roped-off area of the flat, smooth parking lot. A fifteen-foot length of two-inch pipe had been set up about a foot off the ground. Jumps made from planks resting on plastic blocks piled two and three high were scattered about. In the center of the roped-off area was an actual fire hydrant Dan Lyons had bought from the city of San Carlos. It was welded to a thick steel plate.

Petey made a slow circuit without doing anything, skating the nervousness out of his system.

"This dude is nothin' but heavy on the streets," Mike McGee told the crowd. "Petey and I go way back—we've been tight for a long time. During that time, I've seen him come from a shaky fresh cut to a real power in freestyling. Some of you probably heard what Petey did out at the unfinished highway not too far from here. It was purely awesome! I can't go into specifics right now, but the dude showed a lot of heart!"

Petey ran hard at a high jump and laid an olly that cleared the board by a solid foot and a half. He touched down sweetly, all four wheels kissing the pavement at the same time. He beamed when the applause hit him. His board felt good, he felt good, and he was ready to do some radical freestyling. The crowd suddenly disappeared from Petey's world. He was alone with his skateboard—and the street.

He wheeled toward the fire hydrant like an express train and tromped the tail of his board, launching himself at it. He heard a solid thunk as the center of his board banged onto the top of the hydrant. He used his momentum and a quick snap of his body to turn his board and himself into a propeller. The audience roared as he dropped back to the pavement, shot over a low jump, and powered toward the rail.

"Here's a move my friend Petey is famous for," Mike McGee told the audience. "Maybe you've seen some grinds before—but you haven't seen a power grind until you've seen Petey Marino bag one!"

Petey sped toward the rail. He kicked his board up exactly as high as it needed to be and not an iota more, saving all his speed. His front trucks were up—and then his rear trucks. Metal scraped against metal as Petey shot the full length of the fifteen-foot rail. The applause from the stands was deafening.

He dropped back to the pavement with enough speed left to slide his board around in a tight, fast 360. He pushed out of the 360, swung into another turn, jammed down the tail of his board, and skidded to a stop. Then he stepped off the deck, tromped on the tail again, and snatched the board out of midair like a trained dog catching a treat.

The whoops and cheers that followed let Petey

know exactly how well his routine had gone over. The Wizards rushed him, joined by Burnhart, Heidi, Chelsea and lots of others.

The Street Wizards stood in a tight bunch watching the other freestylers. Then Tom and Jordan went to get soft drinks for the four of them. Petey chewed on his lower lip as he watched the rest of the routines.

Lance Trevor, of Digger, stepped up behind Bobby and put his hand on the boy's shoulder. "I want to talk with you," he said.

Bobby nodded. "OK, but I want my friend Petey to hear what you have to say, too."

"Your pal can wait, Bobby. I need to talk to you in private. This is business—sponsorship business."

"We can talk right here, Mr. Trevor," Bobby insisted. "Petey's a Street Wizard, just like I am. He can hear whatever it is you have to say."

Mr. Trevor sighed. "OK, kid," he finally agreed. "I've been thinking about our talk earlier, and I've made my decision. I've got a contract right here in my pocket for you to take home and show your parents. Digger Shoes is ready to sign you up now."

"You won't need that contract. Thanks for the offer—but no thanks. You've got Corey Burnhart, and we may just have a sponsor of our own— someone from San Carlos who's behind *all* of us."

"Who is it?" Mr. Trevor asked. "I assure you Digger can top any offer that . . ."

"You don't understand," Bobby interrupted. "I guess I just don't dig some of the things that seem to go with having a heavy sponsor."

"What are you talking about, kid?"

"Look, I heard the way you were ordering Corey Burnhart around. It's obvious that skating isn't number one with you guys."

Mr. Trevor started to respond, but instead simply looked at Bobby, with obvious disbelief. "Why . . . why, you're nuts, kid. Plain nuts!" he finally said. "Thousands and thousands of kids would give anything for an offer like I've made you!"

Bobby and Petey began to turn away when Mr. Trevor stepped up next to Petey. "Hey, aren't you the freestyle hero? Maybe we can work something out. Let's talk about it and . . ."

Petey smiled at the man. "No, thanks. The Street Wizards are kind of a funny group—sign one of us and you got to sign us all. See, we're just too busy digging skating and hanging with each other to hype sneakers."

Mr. Trevor looked stunned. Petey and Bobby walked over to where Tom and Jordan were waiting for them by the freestyle area. The last skater had finished his moves. The audience was quiet and still as Mike McGee prepared to read the names of the winners in Radlands' Megarad competition.

"First, the ramp results," Mike announced, milking all the drama out of the moment. "An honorable mention goes to—Bobby Clark and Tom Garcia for their dynamite crossover vert!"

Petey and Jordan cheered their buddies, along with the entire crowd. Silence fell as McGee announced the ramp winner—Corey Burnhart. Corey accepted his trophy and had his picture taken with the Lion, whose sponsor, Mega Boards, had him hustling around to have his picture taken with every skater who placed in the competition. After the applause had died down, Mike McGee gave a short plug for his show, then set out to announce the winners of the freestyle competition.

"Honorable mention—and this is going to come as a surprise to some people—goes to Lisa Franklin, a lady freestyler from San Diego who makes pavement scream! I've known Lisa ever since . . ."

The applause covered the rest of Mike's line. Bobby, Tom, Jordan, and Petey waited, not saying a word. Petey shifted from foot to foot with pent-up tension, wishing McGee would quit running his mouth and announce third place. Bobby noticed his friend's nervousness.

The baddest emcee cleared his throat and looked down at his piece of paper. Then he refolded it and put it in his pocket. The crowd was hushed, with all eyes riveted on him. He picked up the third-place trophy, pretended to rub some dust off it, then set it back down on the awards table. He stood looking at it for a moment and then turned back to the crowd.

"This trophy is in the way up here. There must be some way to get rid of it. Hey! I've got it. I'll give the silly thing away." He pretended to think for a moment, then said, "Petey Marino—you got room for this on your folks' mantelpiece?"

Mike McGee's voice boomed as he proclaimed, "Third place winner in the freestyle competition— Petey Marino, one hot skater. It's all yours, good buddy! Congratulations!"

The audience erupted more loudly than they had all afternoon. Word about Petey's saving Brad Munson's hide had gotten around very quickly. But no one cheered more loudly than the Street Wizards as Petey walked up to accept his trophy.

When Petey came back to the Wizards, an older man was standing with Bobby, Jordan, and Tom. Mike McGee was announcing the other winners in the freestyle competition, but none of the Wizards were paying attention.

"Hey, Petey," Jordan called out. "This is Mr. Trumble, from the video-and-computer store, who was thinking about sponsoring us."

Trumble gave Petey a big smile. "I just made your friends an offer."

Petey shot Bobby a quick look. "I thought . . . but with Digger . . . ?"

"Forget Digger Sneaks," Bobby said. "Mr. Trumble says he really likes the ramp skating Tom and I are doing. But your freestyling really blows him away."

Mr. Trumble nodded. "That's right, Petey. Especially that power grind you did out there. So the deal is this—T-shirts and safety gear, and my store will pay your way to the statewide championships in Sacramento next month."

"And we have total freedom to choose our own routines," Tom announced, glancing at Mr. Trumble for confirmation.

He nodded. "What do you say, Petey?"

The four Street Wizards were grinning at each other. For weeks they had known that if they placed in this competition, they would be eligible for the statewide one. But they never expected to go; they couldn't afford it, and while their parents approved of their having fun on their skateboards, *they* weren't going to sponsor them as pros. "This is unreal," Petey said, beaming and putting out his fist with a big, fat thumbs-up sign.

"It almost is," Bobby said, slapping his arm around Petey's back. With Mr. Trumble they were getting the best of both worlds—a sponsor as well as the freedom to choose their own moves.

Now Jordan and Tom joined Petey and Bobby for a huddle. They broke out of it cheering and showering thanks on Mr. Trumble.

"Don't worry about it," Mr. Trumble said. "We skaters have to stick together. All I ask is that next month in Sacramento, you guys skate even hotter than you did today."

The Street Wizards had a sponsor—and a lot of work to do!

BE A RAD RIDER, LEARN TO DO A GRIND!

"Grinding" is a trick that both freestyle and ramp skaters do. A grind is what you do when you slide your board along the edge of something by skidding on the trucks. Freestyle skaters grind on curbs or rails, while ramp skaters like to grind on the coping, which is the concrete or metal edge at the top of the ramp. Grinding is a three-part trick. Here's how a freestyler would grind a curb:

1. Approach the curb from a slight angle, and just before you reach it stomp down hard on the tail of your board. This will kick the nose up onto the curb.

2. Make sure the top edge of the curb meets the front truck—the metal part between your two front wheels. The rear part of your board is below the edge. Or with practice, you can put both trucks on the edge, which is called a "fifty-fifty." Now start sliding! That's a power grind!

3. The tricky part is finishing your grind. Stomp down on the tail to raise the nose of your board and free the truck from the edge of the curb. Just when the nose is high enough, turn your board quickly in the direction you want to go.

You can do a frontside grind or a backside grind. Once you've mastered the basics, the fun part is learning to grind as long as possible. Some of the champs can power grind for almost twenty feet! Hot stuff!

LISTEN UP!

Make sure skateboarding is a safe sport. When you're working on those aggro moves, *always* wear your safety equipment—kneepads, elbowpads, and a good-quality plastic helmet.

Live long and prosper!